RESURRECTION FROM
THE UNDERGROUND

FEODOR
DOSTOEVSKY

RESURRECTION FROM THE UNDERGROUND

FEODOR DOSTOEVSKY

RENÉ GIRARD

Edited and Translated by
James G. Williams

A Crossroad Herder Book
The Crossroad Publishing Company
New York

1997

The Crossroad Publishing Company
370 Lexington Avenue, New York, NY 10017

Printed in the United States of America

Library of Congress Cataloging-in-Publication Data

Girard, René, 1923-
    [Dostoïevski, du double à l'unité. English]
    Resurrection from the underground : Feodor Dostoevsky / René
Girard : translated and foreword by James G. Williams.
       p. cm.
    "A Crossroad Herder book."
    Includes bibliographical references (p.) and index.
    ISBN: 0-8245-1608-7
    1. Dostoyevsky, Fyodor, 1821-1881 – Criticism and interpretation.
I. Title.
PG3328.Z6G4913 1997
891.73'3 – dc21
                                          96-28582
                                            CIP

Contents

Foreword

René Girard

by James G. Williams

The Man and the Controversy

From one perspective René Girard has lived a quiet, un-
eventful life. But viewed from another angle, it has been a
life of daring and courage. One view is that of the professor
and family man, married for forty-five years, father of three
children, grandfather of seven. For years he has followed
the routine of rising at 3:30 a.m., working in his study until
noon, and, until retirement in 1995, teaching or seeing students in the afternoon. Yet during the entire period of his
career he has defied the intellectual fashions swirling about
him. With his first two books, *Deceit, Desire, and the Novel*
and this one, *Resurrection from the Underground: Feodor
Dostoevsky,** he rejected the literary retreat of the 1950s
and early 1960s from concern with history, society, and the
psyche. However, his first two books did not scandalize the
intellectual world. They seemed to stay within a literary
context, and they focused on desire, which enjoyed a vogue
by the 1960s. In these initial writings he analyzed the work

---

*All of Girard's books are listed in the bibliography. The information about
the original French edition is presented after the English-language data. Girard's study of Shakespeare is the exception among his books: he wrote it in
English, so the English is the original, but the French translation was published first. For a full bibliography of all Girard's writings, see *The Girard
Reader,* ed. James G. Williams (New York: Crossroad, 1996), 295–302.

of Cervantes, Stendahl, Flaubert, Proust, and Dostoevsky in terms of "triangular" or "mimetic" desire: our desires are copied from models or mediators whose objects of desire become our objects of desire. But the model or mediator we imitate can become our rival if we desire precisely the object he is imagined to have. Or other imitators of the same model may compete with us for the same objects. Jealousy and envy are inevitably aroused in this mimetic situation.

But to this point Girard was seldom attacked. He was yet fully to develop his inference from the great novels that the role of Christianity, particularly Christ and the Gospels, was and continues to be central to the dynamics of Western culture, and it took him several more years to conceive and formulate his thesis that human culture begins with violence and scapegoating.

But in the 1970s the situation changed, and Girard's professional life became one of renown and notoriety, particularly in France, where the work of intellectuals was widely read and subject to radio and television interviews. Four of Girard's books were published during this decade, but the two that attracted all the attention were *Violence and the Sacred* and *Things Hidden since the Foundation of the World*. *Violence and the Sacred*, which was generally well received, argues that mimetic desire leads to violence, from which the sacred emerges. Mimetic desire is the human phenomenon of learning to desire, and what to desire, through imitating some other person's desire. To the extent that anyone desires an object, there is potential for conflict and violence if the desiring person competes with the mediator of desire for the object. Likewise, the probability of conflict and violence is increased if two or more persons under the mimetic influence of the mediator seek to acquire the object. The sacred is a management of violence by a partial and distorted representation of the original violence. The unintended effect of the sacred is social order.

It was really the publication of *Things Hidden* which startled, shocked, and in some instances simply pleased or excited readers in France. In this work he further consolidated the anthropological basis of his theory and extended its psychological implications. But the heart of the book, right at the center of its format and central to its argument, is the thesis that the biblical revelation, the disclosure of "things hidden since the foundation of the world," is the key to understanding human violence, human history, and human knowledge. What had been hidden in culture and its formation through the sacred was the violence done to victims and camouflaged in prohibition, ritual, and myth. The sacred as violence is demythologized in the tendency of biblical narratives to side with the victim against the persecuting community and in the biblical witness to the God of victims. This exposure of sacred violence and affirmation of the God who sides with victims is fully realized in the Gospel texts, in which Christ is the perfect revelation of the innocent victim.

Girard's interdisciplinary approach and Christian vision affirming the truth of the Bible fly directly in the face of the great currents of anti-Christian thought emerging from the nineteenth century, particularly those associated with Karl Marx, Friedrich Nietzsche, and Sigmund Freud, with which the trendiest intellectuals are still enamored and which, as mediated through latter-day epigoni, have even become a kind of negative canon in many religious studies departments and theological seminaries. However, Girard has quietly persisted in the midst of all the controversy and largely ignored the sometimes abusive, frequently ignorant things said and written about him. In his own writings he is often polemical, but very seldom is this polemic *ad hominem.*

In three other books since the 1970s, plus a set of interviews by Michel Treguer,* Girard has continued to extend and refine all the themes of his earlier work, but with a growing emphasis on its religious aspect and the need to respond to those who attack Christianity as their main scapegoat and accuse the Gospels of being the primary Western source of prejudice, scapegoating, and demonization of enemies. He has engaged in constant argument with Freud and the Freudian tradition, Lévi-Strauss and structuralism, and various French "postmodernists." He largely rejects deconstruction, multiculturalism, and everything associated with "political correctness." A thinker more alienated from current intellectual fashions, yet more positive and optimistic concerning human possibilities under God, could scarcely be imagined.

Girard's Engagement with Dostoevsky

It is widely accepted that few writers, if any, analyze envy, shame, and sadomasochistic relationships better than Dostoevsky did in his novels and short stories. In his writings he revealed resentment in a vividness and depth that were to make even Nietzsche marvel, and his narrative probing of obsession with the model-mediator of desire is brilliant. His works are a literary laboratory of this most basic dimension of social psychology, which could also be described as mimetic psychology or even mimetic anthropology. For

---

*See bibliography.

Girard, Dostoevsky was one of the wondrous discoveries
of his work in literature. Early in his career he turned to
the work of Dostoevsky, both as one of the sources of
his mimetic model and a body of texts to illustrate his
argument.

Resurrection from the Underground: Feodor Dostoevsky,
first published in 1963, is the only lengthy essay or book-
length work by Girard that has not been previously translated into English. The fiction of Dostoevsky was very important for Girard's argument for "novelistic truth" against
"romantic deception" in *Deceit, Desire, and the Novel.* It
was Dostoevsky above all among the novelists who de-
constructed the romantic concept of a spontaneous desire
unrelated to models or mediators and the romantic dream
of a perfect love and a perfectly noble soul separated from
jealousy, envy, conflict, and violence. In this short book
on Dostoevsky Girard extended and refined the argument
mounted in his first book. His deep involvement with Dostoevsky was an important stage on the way toward what
would become his full thesis, that the origin of human culture is a process of sacralizing violence, which the Jewish
and Christian revelation would call into question.

This book is especially important because it brings together the two sides of Girard's approach since the late
1950s, the mimetic-literary and the religious. He was inspired by Dostoevsky not merely to *allow* his Christian faith
into his research, but to dare to see the Christian revelation—the Gospels in particular—as its very foundation.

He argues that the best commentary on Dostoevsky's earlier fiction is his later work, especially the great novels,
and that Dostoevsky himself attained a spiritual understanding and personal integration which is not completely

exemplified in any one of his great characters, but which
he found and developed through creating these very fictional characters. Dostoevsky's creative work is shown to
be simultaneously a personal journey of attaining a whole,
unified self and a commentary on Russia's social and cultural crisis, which included the preoccupation of Russian
intellectuals with the cutting edges of European culture.
Dostoevsky depicted the crisis of modernism, prophetically
anticipating all the issues associated with "postmodernism."
He exposed the contradictions of nihilism and socialism,
sometimes in ways which come across as critiques composed in the second half of the twentieth century.

What Girard does, in effect, is to review Dostoevsky's
own journey from the underground. This "underground" is
associated with Dostoevsky's obsessive character in *Notes
from the Underground*. It is existence, typically modern,
which is riddled with resentment of models who are at the
same time rivals and obstacles to the individual. Underground people are imitators who try to hide their imitation
from others, and even from themselves. Those at the extreme of underground existence, leading an "addicted" life,
are attracted to those who spurn them and spurn those
who are attracted to them. (See Girard's Postface, especially
pp. 147, 152.)

To accomplish this review, Girard recounts Dostoevsky's
passage into the "inferno" of unrecognized masochism and
romanticism, through the "underground psychology" of
alienation and resentment and the "underground metaphysics" of idolatrous obsession with the all-powerful
model or mediator, and shows that these are all stages
leading toward a spiritual healing, a "resurrection." This
process is detectable in his literary works as a whole.

A Note on This Translation

The translation posed few problems and has been carefully reviewed by Girard himself. I am grateful also to Cesáreo Bandera for reading it carefully and offering both corrections and suggestions for improvement. A biographical prologue on Dostoevsky has been added for the English translation so that the reader may follow the discussion of Dostoevsky and his work without extensive prior knowledge about him and his historical context.

As was to be expected, there were some words in the French text which could not be easily rendered with precision into English. Of these, two are significant enough to mention here. A word appearing quite frequently in the French text is *dédoublement,* "dividing into two, duplicating," and often its verb occurs, *dédoubler,* "divide." In context, *dédoublement* almost always refers to division of the self, the emergence of the "double." I have therefore usually translated the noun as "self-division."

The other word occurs less frequently but is also very important, particularly in the last chapter: *rassembler,* "gather, collect." The subtitle of the French edition is "du double à l'unité," from the double to unity, which indicates the thesis of the monograph. The English title, *Resurrection from the Underground,* points to the same thesis viewed from the standpoint of a larger narrative pattern. It follows the structure of the drama of the Incarnation of Christ, which Girard clarifies toward the end of the book as the structure of Dostoevsky's novelistic journey. *Rassembler* is the verb that Girard employs to describe Dostoevsky's method of gathering, of bringing the doubled self and alienated individuals together again through a vision of a new, resurrected humanity, especially in *The Brothers Karamazov*. Girard says, "But to master [the dialectic of pride] something other than intelligence is required. It requires a victory over pride itself. The proud intellect will never comprehend the saying of Christ: 'Whoever does not gather [*rassemble*] with me scatters' [Matthew 12:30/Luke 11:23]." My point in mentioning this is that I tried to stay with the basic sense of "gather" in the last chapter, but Girard uses *rassembler* occasionally prior to the last chapter in contexts where I did not think I could translate it with that word. Unfortunately, a certain sense of the unity of the argument is lost which one would otherwise gain through knowing the key words of the French text.

One way to remedy this would be to put French words in parentheses or to add notes on the text. But one of Girard's fundamental axioms in writing is not to allow language to call attention to itself. In this regard, his approach is once again the antithesis of much writing described as "deconstructionist" and "postmodern." Although he acknowledges the relativity of language and the continual problem of displacement and representation, particularly because of myth and an unrecognized scapegoat mechanism, he believes that we are not left to flounder in a completely unredeemed world of language. There is a truth which founds language and pulls it toward its own origin and end. Thus, although it is valid to reflect on words and to use word-plays, the self-indulgence that continually calls attention to itself and the desirability of its own intellectual game is an example once more of the pride of intellect that scatters rather than gathers.

Chronology of
Feodor Dostoevsky

1821   Born October 30 in Moscow to Mikhail Andree-
           vich and Maria Feodorovna.

1836   Dostoevsky's mother dies.

1838   Dostoevsky enters Academy of Military Engi-
           neering, Petersburg.

1839   Dostoevsky's father dies, purportedly murdered
           by peasants.

1843   Passes his final examinations; resigns his army
           commission in 1844.

1845   Belinsky praises *Poor Folk;* Dostoevsky cele-
           brated even before it is published.

1846   *Poor Folk; The Double,* which was attacked
           by Belinsky. Dostoevsky not to regain literary
           renown until 1860.

1847–49   Writes for newspaper, composes short stories, in-
           cluding "The Landlady," "White Nights," and
           "A Weak Heart." Works on unfinished novel,
           Netotchka Nezvanova. Becomes involved with
           a group of socialist thinkers, the "Petrashevsky
           Circle"; is arrested in 1849. Sentenced to death,
           faces a mock execution with several others. Sen-

tence altered to four years of penal servitude in Omsk (Siberia).

1850–54   In prison. When released in 1854 he is made to serve as a private in the Seventh Line Battalion at Semipalatinsk (eventually promoted to non-commissioned officer). Through friendship with Baron Wrangel he meets his future wife.

1857   Marries Maria Dmitrievna, who had become a widow.

1858   He writes *The Village of Stepanchikova* and "Uncle's Dream."

1859   After ten years' exile, returns to Petersburg with his wife.

1860   *The Insulted and Injured* and *The House of the Dead,* the latter a memoir of his prison experiences, notable for the realistic and sympathetic treatment of the convicts he knew. Published first in *Time,* a literary journal of which he had become editor.

1863   Maria Dmitrievna seriously ill. Dostoevsky goes abroad (the second time since his return from exile), forms a liaison with Appollinaria Prokofievna Suslova.

1864   His wife dies in April and his elder brother, to whom he was very close, dies in July. Writes *Notes from the Underground,* an important book in Western literature, one foreshadowing the writer's great works to come.

1865   Flees Russia to escape his debts, gambles and loses at Wiesbaden. Writes *Crime and Punishment.*

1866   *Crime and Punishment.*

1867   *The Gambler.* Marries Anna Grigorievna Snikina, the stenographer to whom he dictated *The Gambler* in one month. They flee Russia to avoid creditors and the pressure of his importunate relatives. They were to live abroad for four years.

1868   A daughter, Sofya, is born, but dies after five months. Dostoevsky writes *The Idiot;* they move to Italy.

1869   Lyubov, a daughter, born in Dresden. Family in great poverty. Dostoevsky much interested in Russian news accounts about student disorders and a revolutionary group led by Sergey Nechaev. Nechaev linked with the murder of a student. Dostoevsky refashioned and adapted this material for *Demons.*

1870   Franco-Prussian War. Dostoevsky and wife long to return to Russia. *The Eternal Husband.* Works on *Demons.*

1871   Dostoevsky stops gambling. Return to Russia. *Demons* published. A son, Feodor, born in Petersburg.

1873   Becomes editor of *The Citizen,* resigns in 1874. Begins publishing *The Diary of a Writer.*

1875   *A Raw Youth.* Long troubled by emphysema, he
            goes to Ems for a cure, winters in Staraya Russa.
            A son, Aleksey, is born.

1876–77   *The Diary of a Writer,* installments in *The Citi-
            zen.* "A Gentle Creature" and "The Dream of a
            Ridiculous Man."

1878   Works on *The Brothers Karamazov.* Aleksey
            dies.

1880   *The Brothers Karamazov.* Dostoevsky speaks at
            unveiling of monument to Pushkin, is wildly
            acclaimed.

1881   Dies on January 28.

A Biographical Prologue

For Dostoevsky scholars and those who are familiar with his work and historical context, this brief biographical sketch will not be necessary. For any other readers, however, it should be read before proceeding to this study of Dostoevsky. The basic biographical context for understanding *Resurrection from the Underground* is given here. The reader may also consult the chronology of Dostoevsky's life.

Feodor Mikhailovich Dostoevsky's early circumstances were not of the sort to allow one to predict a literary career, let alone the career of a writer for whom "genius," or some similar epithet, could be appropriately used. Born in 1821 in Moscow, he was the middle child of three children born to Mikhail Andreevich and Maria Feodorovna Dostoevsky. His father was a medical doctor who worked for many years in a hospital for the poor; his mother was the daughter of a merchant family. The father was concerned for the education of his children and not an unkindly man, but he was evidently very rigid and prone to outbursts of anger. The mother was attractive and lively, known far and wide in the area where the Dostoevskys owned a landed estate for her compassion to the poor. Both parents were very religious. Dostoevsky's father seems to have understood himself as specially chosen and led by God, although his worldly attainments did not bring him the status he believed he deserved.

The death of their parents must have deeply affected Feodor and his brother and sister. Maria Feodorovna died in 1836 when Feodor was only fifteen. Before she died she called for an icon of the Savior and blessed her children and husband. This scene must have remained vivid in Feodor's memory and is probably reflected in a number of deathbed scenes in his works.

Dostoevsky's father died in 1839. In fact, it was believed that he was killed by peasants who worked for him and who revolted in anger because of his tirades and mistreatment of them. It now appears that he was not murdered. But this rumor was believed by all the family, including Feodor, so the effect was the same for him.

In 1838, at the behest of his father, Dostoevsky entered a school of military engineering in St. Petersburg. He was extremely unhappy there most of the time. However, he did well enough to pass the more professionally oriented courses, and he excelled in humanistic studies, especially languages (French and German) and literature. From his childhood he had been inspired by Pushkin, whose artistry was associated especially with Petersburg. Gogol lived and worked in Petersburg for most of his adult years, and Dostoevsky became interested in his stories while at the military academy.

He graduated from the military academy in 1843. But his ambition for many years had been to become a writer, so in 1844 he resigned his army commission and began writing *Poor Folk*. He himself was as poor as could be, utterly naive in the ways of the literary world and taken completely by surprise by the praise and social popularity that burst forth even before the publication of *Poor Folk* in 1846. Its favorable reception was due primarily to the enthusiastic endorsement given it by Visarion Belinsky, the eminent Russian literary critic of the time, who was a liberal with socialist tendencies. Basking in the light of Belinsky's approval, Dostoevsky was lionized for a short while, but soon the literary culture of Petersburg turned against him because of his awkward manners and naive, arrogant obsession with himself. When *The Double* was published late in 1846, Belinsky did not like its more psychological orientation and cut him off completely. He had, as it were, given birth to him as a literary figure, and he killed the immediate career of his protégé just as quickly.

Following his break with the Belinsky circle, Dostoevsky continued his work as a writer. He experimented with literary form and composed some interesting short stories, including "The Landlady," "White Nights," and "A Weak Heart." Turning away from the liberal literary set, he became involved with a group of revolutionary socialist thinkers, the "Petrashevsky Circle," who studied the French socialists and discussed the need for social and political reform in Russia. A wave of reaction resulted in the arrest of the Petrashevsky group in 1849. Those tried and convicted were sentenced to death. A mock execution ensued which made a lasting impression on Dostoevsky and to which he alluded several times in his later work, most notably in *The Idiot*. Dostoevsky's sentence was altered to four years of penal servitude in Omsk (Siberia). His attacks of epilepsy probably date to his first year in prison.

He served his prison sentence from 1850 to 1854. His experiences in prison profoundly changed his life. The one book that he was allowed to possess was a New Testament which had been given to him as a gift. Through his meditation on the New Testament, which he read frequently, and his reflections on other prisoners and his relations with them, he was converted decisively to a Christianity centered in the loving and compassionate Christ.

When he was released he was not allowed to return to Russia as a civilian. He was made instead to serve for five years in the army. He began as a private in the Seventh Line Battalion at Semipalatinsk and was eventually promoted to the rank of non-commissioned officer. Through a young lawyer, Baron Alexander Wrangel, who was to become his friend and confidante, he met the Isaev family and fell in love with the wife, Maria Dmitrievna Isaeva. When Alexander Isaev died, Dostoevsky was able finally to marry the widow, though not without an ambivalent struggle to keep her from marrying another suitor. This ambivalence will be discussed in the following study of Dostoevsky's work and creativity. The marriage took place in 1857; it was an unhappy one from the first.

During the last few years in Siberia Dostoevsky began writing again. *The Village of Stepanchikova* was published in 1859. It was in 1859 that he returned to Petersburg with his wife and stepson, after ten years of exile. His relations with his wife seem to have become chronically strained, and, to make matters worse, it was soon apparent that she suffered from tuberculosis. However, he published two works in 1860 which brought him to public notice once more and portended the literary success he would finally attain. One was the novel, *The Insulted and Injured*. It is a story that reflects some of the preoccupations of romanticism and is often melodramatic. However, it shows the writer as more than ever the master of love triangles, and its dominant character, Prince Volkovsky, was to foreshadow later sinister, proud characters in Dostoevsky's fiction, most notably

Stavrogin in *Demons* and Versilov in *A Raw Youth*. The other book was a memoir of his four years in the Siberian prison, *The House of the Dead*. Its realistic description of the prisoners and prison conditions attracted much public comment.

Dostoevsky began to travel in Europe. During his second trip, in 1863, he met and formed a liaison with Appollinaria Prokofievna Suslova. He dominated her at first, but eventually she broke from him and made him intensely jealous by taking another lover. She was probably the model of several proud, imperious women in the novels, especially Nastaya Filippovna in *The Idiot*.

The year 1864 was crucial in Dostoevsky's life. His wife died in April. Then in July his brother Mikhail, to whom he was very close, died suddenly. His attempts to pay off his brother's debts and aid his family financially drove the writer himself further into debt. He also wanted to provide for his stepson, "Pasha," who became a rather shiftless young man always begging for and expecting money from his stepfather.

But 1864 was a signal year because *Notes from the Underground* was published. It was an immediate failure in that the literary world took almost no notice of it. But it was to become one of his best known works. This was the first — and one of the very few — books by Dostoevsky that Nietzsche read. Nietzsche found in it the epitome of his concept of resentment, the sublimated desire that stems from envy of the powerful and finds its satisfaction in deferred revenge. The underground man embodies a reaction against utilitarian rationalism, but he is also bitingly satirized for his petty resentments, fantasies of revenge, and inability really to love another person.

To escape his debts and importunate relatives, Dostoevsky fled from Russia in 1865. He found himself even more deeply in debt because of a compulsion to gamble. But he managed to write *Crime and Punishment,* which was published in 1866. Its protagonist, Raskolnikov, is the first of the characters clearly embodying the idea of the man-god, the person who finds meaning only in the affirmation of the absolute autonomy of the individual, as contrasted to the characters embodying the God-man, the Christ-figures whose individuality gathers others about them in loving community.

In 1866 Dostoevsky began writing *The Gambler.* He decided, with some foreboding, to hire a stenographer to whom he could dictate the book in a hurry. To his good fortune, the stenographer turned out to be Anna Grigorievna Snikina, who was only eighteen years old (Dostoevsky was forty-five), but already a person of maturity, intelligence, and a good education for Russian women of that time. Within a short period the relationship became more than professional, and they were married in 1867. Their marriage was to see him through many difficult experiences, and her understanding with regard to his gambling addiction was doubtlessly a primary factor in his eventual ability to give it up.

The Gambler appeared in 1867. It is usually taken as a study of the character of Russians, particularly their desire to emulate the success, knowledge, and refinement of western Europeans, but it is also a fine narrative study of the relation between romantic infatuation and addiction to gambling. Meanwhile, Dostoevsky's debts were piling up and some of the relatives, above all Pasha, were imposing themselves more than ever. It appears that in this situation, which must have become increasingly uncomfortable for the young wife, Anna Dostoevsky herself argued that they should live abroad for awhile. They left Russia, but were to stay away much longer than they expected. They did not return until 1871.

Thus began four years of sojourning in various cities and countries, usually in Germany. The couple were often at extremities due to poverty and were racked at times by Dostoevsky's epilepsy and gambling problem, but somehow they managed to exist and Dostoevsky found strength to write. Two daughters were born in this self-imposed exile, only one of whom survived, Lyubov, born in Dresden in 1869.

He wrote and published one of the greatest of his novels during this period, *The Idiot*. He had conceived the project of writing the story of "a perfectly beautiful man" whose life would be contrasted to the story of "a great sinner." These two characters were perhaps initially to be part of one story, but they bifurcated into two, *The Idiot* and *Demons*. The main character in *The Idiot*, Prince Myshkin, who is innocent and loving, and ostensibly wants to look for the good in everyone, turns out to be deeply ambiguous. The reader is left with the question of whether Myshkin does more harm than good to those around him. The novel is commonly described as uneven and badly plotted. Be that as it may, it is perhaps Dostoevsky's most original novel. He had become more and more conservative politically and socially and could blaze in anger against various forms of nihilism, socialism, and the desire to ape western European manners and institutions. But in this work he subjects his own cherished ideas and convictions, as embodied in Myshkin, to searching criticism.

By contrast to *The Idiot*, the next novel, *The Eternal Husband*, is short and elegantly plotted. Through a juxtaposition of the main character and narrator, Velchaninov, to his rival who comes seeking him out, Trusotsky, Dostoevsky created a fascinating tale centered in the rivalry and conflict engendered by mimetic desire. The "eternal husband," Trusotsky, desires revenge from the "eternal lover," Velchaninov, who had had an affair with Trusotsky's now deceased wife. At the same, Trusotsky is dependent on Velchaninov and needs his approval, even his love.

In 1869, Dostoevsky was very interested in Russian news accounts about student disorders and a revolutionary group led by Sergey Nechaev. Nechaev was eventually linked with the murder of a student. Dostoevsky refashioned, adapted, and of course greatly expanded and supplemented this material for *Demons*, which was published after the Dostoevskys returned to Russian in 1871. It is surely one of the greatest critiques of atheist revolutionary movements ever written, but it is so valuable because of the way in which the author was able to flesh out his ideas in memorable characters: Stavrogin ("cross-bearer"), the charismatic but pathologically empty star to whom everyone looks for wisdom and power, though in fact whatever content his character has is filled in by his followers, who are possessed by the "demons" of atheistic ideologies; Stepan Verkhovensky, the dilettante intellectual from the 1840s whose insipid imitation of everything European amounted to participation in the loosing of the demons on the people; Peter Verkhovensky, the son of Stepan whose sinister, mercurial character was partially modeled after Nechaev; and a number of others besides these.

The last nine or ten years of Dostoevsky's life, after the

return to Russia, were a period of greater professional and financial security. Anna played no little part in this; besides sharing marital love with her husband and caring for the household, she oversaw the household finances and even took a hand in selling his books. He made one last visit to Wiesbaden in 1871. He sent to Anna for more money, but promised after this last fling he would give up gambling. It sounded like previous promises, but this time he did it. Two more children, both sons, were born, but only one of them, Feodor, survived. So the Dostoevskys had two children, a daughter and a son, who lived into adulthood. He published his notes, *The Diary of a Writer,* over several years, and wrote *A Raw Youth* and, of course, *The Brothers Karamazov* (1880). Whether *The Brothers Karamazov* is the best of his great novels, it is the crowning one. It gathers together, as Girard points out, the anguished, resentful, alienated individuals and the hopes for a better world for which the various atheistic ideologies had yearned, and joins them together in the transforming vision of a new, resurrected humanity. This transforming, all-embracing vision overflowed into his wildly acclaimed speech on Pushkin, which was given late in 1880.

Although epilepsy was the malady that affected Dostoevsky in many ways and on which he drew in his writing (especially in *The Idiot*), he was a heavy cigarette smoker and suffered for the last decade of his life from emphysema. He died January 28, 1881. On January 25 and 26 he was seized with bouts of coughing up blood. On the 26th a priest was called so that he could confess and receive Communion. He seemed to improve on the 27th, but the next day he was taken worse and died in the evening.

RESURRECTION FROM
THE UNDERGROUND

FEODOR
DOSTOEVSKY

Chapter 1

Descent into the Inferno

Contemporary critics readily say that writers create themselves in creating their work. This formula is eminently applicable to Dostoevsky as long as one does not confuse this twofold creative process with the acquisition of a technique or even with the perfect mastery of a field or subject.

One should not compare the author's successive works to the musical exercises by which musicians gradually increase their virtuosity. What is essential lies elsewhere and cannot be expressed initially except in a negative form. For Dostoevsky, to create oneself is to slay the old human state, prisoner as it is of aesthetic, psychological, and spiritual forms that shrink his horizon as a man and a writer. The disorder, the interior degradation, the very blindness that the earlier works reflect in their totality, present a striking contrast to the lucidity of the works after *The Insulted and Injured;* this is particularly true of the inspired and serene vision of *The Brothers Karamazov.*

Dostoevsky and his work are exemplary, not in the sense of a corpus of work and a life without fault, but in exactly the opposite sense. In observing this author live and write we learn, perhaps, that peace of soul is the most difficult of conquests and that genius is not a natural phenomenon. From the quasi-legendary image of a repentant convict we should retain the idea of this twofold redemption, but we should retain nothing else, for ten long years elapsed between Siberia and the decisive rupture.

From *Notes from the Underground* on, Dostoevsky is no longer content to rehash his old certainties and to justify himself in his own eyes by continuing to take the same point of view about others and about himself. He exorcises his demons, one after the other, by embodying them in his novels. Nearly each book marks a new conversion, and this imposes a new perspective on the perennial problems with which he deals.

Beyond the superficial difference of subjects, all the works form but one; it is this unity that is perceptible to readers when they recognize at first glance a text by Dostoevsky, whatever its date. It is this unity that so many critics seek these days to describe, to possess, to encompass. But to recognize the absolute singularity of the author one admires is not sufficient. Beyond this admiration it is necessary to locate the differences between the particular works, differences which are signs of a quest that may or may not succeed. For Dostoevsky the search for the absolute is not in vain; begun in anxiety, doubt, and deceit, it ends in certitude and joy. It is not by some immutable essence that the writer defines himself but by this exciting itinerary that itself may constitute the greatest of his works. To find its stages it is necessary to compare the individual works and disengage the successive "visions" of Dostoevsky.

The works of genius are based on the destruction of a past which is always more essential, always more original — that is, they are based on the recollection of memories always more distant in time. As the horizon looms larger for the mountain climber, the summit of the mountain becomes nearer. The early works are going to demand of us only a few allusions to attitudes of the writer or to events in his life more or less contemporaneous with their creation. But we will not be able to advance in the master works without turning back again at the same time toward the author's adolescence and infancy through a series of "flashbacks" that may otherwise seem capricious.

The minor violence which we exercise on the early works in order to bring out the obsessive themes will find its justification not in some psychoanalytic or sociological "key," but in the superior lucidity of the master works. It is the writer himself, after all, who will furnish us the point of departure, the orientation, and the instruments of our investigation.

❧

The beginnings of Feodor Mikhailovich Dostoevsky in the literary life were resounding. Belinsky, the most respected of the critics of that epoch, declared that *Poor Folk* was a masterpiece, and he thus quickly made of its author a writer à la mode. Belinsky hailed what we today would call a literature of social commitment, and he saw in the humble resignation of the hero, Makar Devushkin, an indictment of the social order which was even more severe for not having been directly stated.

Makar is a minor government official, poor and already middle-aged. The sole light in his gray and humble existence comes from a young woman, Varenka. He avoids visiting her for fear of scandal-mongering, but he exchanges a quite touching correspondence with her. The "little mother" is not less miserable, sad to say, than her timid protector. She agrees to marry a proprietor who is young and rich but also coarse, brutal, and tyrannical. Makar does not complain;

he does not protest; he does not make the least gesture of revolt. He participates in the preparations for the nuptials; he searches feverishly to make himself useful. He would not recoil from any humiliating expedient, one senses, in order to preserve his modest place in the shadow of his dear Varenka.

A little later, Dostoevsky wrote *The Double,* a work inspired, sometimes rather closely, by certain romantic doubles and above all by *The Nose* of Gogol. *The Double* dominates, from afar and in all instances, all that its author will publish before *Notes from the Underground.* After some ridiculous and humiliating misadventures, the protagonist, Golyadkin, sees his double springing up everywhere he turns, a certain Golyadkin *Junior,* who is physically like him, a functionary like him, occupying the same post as his in the same administrative office. The double treats Golyadkin Senior with a contemptuous disrespect and he thwarts all the bureaucratic and amorous projects into which Golyadkin Senior enters. The appearances of the double multiply, along with the most grotesque failures, to the point that Golyadkin enters an insane asylum.

The biting humor of *The Double* contrasts sharply with the somewhat sickly sweet pathos of *Poor Folk,* but the similarities between the two are more numerous than appear at first glance. Makar Devushkin, like Golyadkin, feels himself always to be martyred by his co-workers. "You know what kills me," he writes to Varenka, "is not the money but all the bothers of life, all those whispers, the faint smiles, the little cutting words." Golyadkin says much the same thing, and the appearance of the double serves only to polarize and concretize his feelings of persecution which remain diffuse and without definite object in his predecessor. Occasionally Golyadkin believes it is possible to make peace with his double. He is then caught up in enthusiasm, imagining the existence he would lead if the spirit of intrigue and cleverness of this maleficent being were in his service rather than mobilized against him. He ponders fusing himself with the double, becoming simply *one* with him — finding, in short, his lost unity. Now the double is to Golyadkin as Varenka's future husband is to Makar Devushkin: the rival, the enemy. So it is fitting to wonder whether the "humble resignation" of Makar, the extraordinary passivity that he demonstrates toward his rival and his pitiful effort to play a small role in the household of the beloved, always in the shadow of the husband, does not stem from an aberration somewhat like that of Golyadkin. Makar certainly has a thousand reasons to flee from a rival much better armed than he is — a thousand reasons, in short, to be obsessed with defeat, and it is from this obsession that Golyadkin suffers. The theme of the double is present in all the works of Dostoevsky in the most diverse and sometimes most hidden forms. Its extensions are so many and ramified that they will not appear to us except little by little.

The "psychological" orientation that is asserted in *The Double* displeased Belinsky. Dostoevsky did not relinquish his obsessions, but he continued to try to express them in a very different form and style. *The Landlady* is an unsuccessful yet significant attempt at romantic frenzy. Ordynov, a melancholy and solitary dreamer, rents a room in the house of a bizarre couple: one a beautiful young woman and the other an enigmatic old man named Murin who exercises an occult power over her. Ordynov falls in love with the "landlady." She declares her love for him also, "like a sister, more than a sister," and eventually she proposes to him that he enter into the enchanted circle of her relations with Murin. The "landlady" desires that these two lovers unite and become one. Ordynov tries to kill his rival, but in vain, for Murin's gaze makes the gun fall from his hands. The idea of the "fusion" of the two protagonists and that of the fascination exercised by Murin may be connected without difficulty to the themes of the preceding works. Once again the subject is defeated by the rival who fascinates him and whose object of desire must be his own.

In *A Weak Heart* we find ourselves once more in the world of minor officials. The story is that of *The Double* but viewed from the outside by an observer who does not share in the hallucinations of the hero. The latter has everything, so it seems, to be happy. His fiancée is charming, his friend is devoted, his superiors are benevolent. But for all that he is no less paralyzed by the possibility of failure, and, like Golyadkin, he sinks little by little into madness.

At an appointed moment the "weak heart" presents his fiancée to his friend, who immediately declares himself in love. Too faithful to compete with his comrade, the "weak heart" asks the latter to make a small place for him in his household. "I love her as much as I love you; she shall be my guardian angel, as for you also. Your happiness will reflect on me and warm me too. May she direct me as she will direct you. From now on my friendship with you and my friendship for her will become one friendship. You will see how she will protect you and how devotedly I will take care of you both." The young woman accepts the idea of a menage à trois with enthusiasm, and she exclaims joyfully, "We three will be one."

The main figure of *White Nights*, as in *The Landlady*, is a "dreamer." He spends the twilight nights of the St. Petersburg summer in long walks. In the course of one of his rambles he makes the acquaintance of a young woman who is no less a romantic dreamer than he, a veritable Russian Emma Bovary. She passed her adolescence attached by a pin to the skirt of her grandmother. He falls in love with her but does not express it because Nastenska expects, at any moment, the return of a young man whom she promised to marry. But she is no longer completely certain that she loves this fiancé. She wonders whether her grandmother's pin is not a bit responsible for this juvenile passion. In the course of an ambiguous exchange of confidences, she accuses her companion of indifference and offers her friendship to him in terms reminiscent of the "landlady" or the fiancée of the "weak heart": "When I get married, we will remain friends, we will be as brother and sister, or even something more. I will love you almost as much as him." The protagonist finally declares his love but, far from pressing his advantage with her, he does everything like Makar Devushkin to insure the success of his rival. He sends the latter Nastenska's letters; he arranges a rendezvous to which he accompanies her. When the two young people meet and fall into each other's arms, he is the fascinated voyeur. The entire conduct of this character is described in terms of generosity, of devotion, of the spirit of sacrifice. Nastenska goes away forever, but she sends to the unfortunate fellow a letter in which she expresses once more what could be called the "dream of the life à trois." "We will see each other again," she writes, "you will come to be with us and you will not leave us. You will be always our friend, my brother."

৵

We know that the young Dostoevsky was paralyzed in the
presence of women, even to the point of fainting when a
well-known St. Petersburg beauty was introduced to him
in a salon. But we know nothing, or nearly nothing, about
a love life which perhaps amounted to very little because
of this paralysis. On the other hand, we are very well
informed about the relationship between Dostoevsky and
Maria Dmitrievna Isaeva, his future wife, during the entire
period that preceded their marriage.

In 1854 Dostoevsky had just got out of prison. He was
not finished with the justice of the czar, for he was required
to enlist in a Siberian regiment and to serve, initially as a
simple soldier, then from 1856 as a subaltern officer. Stationed at Semipalatinsk, he there became a friend of the
Isaev family. The husband, a man intelligent but embittered,
was killing himself with drink. His wife, Maria Dmitrievna,
was thirty years old and spoke much about her ancestors,
French aristocrats who migrated during the French revolution. Seen up close, Semipalatinsk was less a romantic
dream than even the Yonville-l'Abbaye of Madame Bovary.
Greedy minor bureaucrats, brutal soldiers, and adventur-
ers of every sort wallowed there, in the mud or in the
dust according to the season. Maria Dmitrievna immediately inspired feelings in Dostoevsky which any of his heroes
would have experienced: "I fell immediately in love with
the wife of my best friend." What ensued is known to us
from the letters of Feodor Mikhailovich to a young magis-
trate, the aristocratic Wrangel, who did what he could to
mitigate the difficulties of the writer during his years of military service. Very quickly Isaev died. Feodor Mikhailovich
proposed marriage to Maria Dmitrievna, and she did not
refuse. The widow was then living at Kuznetsk, a large vil-

lage even more remote than Semipalatinsk, a real Siberian Dodge City where the role of sheriff was played by the secret police and that of the Indians by the Kirghiz pirates. Naturally Dostoevsky spent all his leaves in Kuznetsk, and it was during one of these trips that tragedy struck. "I saw her," he writes to Wrangel. "What a noble and angelic soul! She cried, she squeezed my hands, but she loves another." *The Other* is named Nikolay Vergunov. He is young and handsome. Feodor Mikhailovich is ugly; he is thirty-five years old and an ex-convict. Like the heroine of *White Nights,* Maria Dmitrievna hesitates. She announces that she is smitten with Vergunov, but she confides in Dostoevsky and encourages him to come see her again.

Vergunov is a teacher. He earns a pittance. If Maria Dmitrievna marries him she would bury herself forever in the remote steppe with a procession of children and a husband too young who would finally leave her. Such is the somber picture that Dostoevsky paints for the widow in his letters. He speaks equally of his brilliant future as a writer, of the fortune awaiting him the day he obtains permission to publish. But very quickly Dostoevsky drops this language; he does not want to compel the proud Maria Dmitrievna to defend her Vergunov. "I don't want to give the impression," he writes, "that I'm working on my own behalf." Pushing the logic of this reasoning to an extreme, he adopts the behavior of his own heroes and makes himself the advocate and supporter of his rival for the young woman. He promises to intervene in his favor with Wrangel. In the letters of this period his writing, which is generally quite clear, occasionally becomes completely illegible. The name of the teacher recurs in his delirious prose like a sort of refrain: "And above all, don't forget Vergunov, for God's sake...."

If the writer sometimes justifies his conduct for tactical reasons, more often he does not hesitate to give himself the finer role. He admires his own grandeur of soul and speaks of himself as he would speak of a hero of Schiller or Jean-Jacques Rousseau. He experiences a "disinterested sympathy" for Vergunov and "compassion" for Maria Dmitrievna. All this "magnanimity" turns out to be rewarding: "I had compassion for her and she inclined toward me — it was for me that she had compassion. You have never known her; at each instant something original, something wise, spiritual, but also paradoxical, infinitely good, truly chivalrous — a knight in woman's dress. She will be lost."

At Kuznetsk they do indeed give themselves over to veritable debauches of chivalry. The two men actually meet. They swear "friendship and fraternity" and fall weeping into each other's arms. Vergunov weeps a lot, and Dostoevsky writes one day to Wrangel that he only knows how to weep. Between two periods of quarreling, Dostoevsky writes feverish letters to obtain for his rival an increase in salary: "Remember, this summer I wrote you on behalf of Vergunov; *he deserves it*." Thus Dostoevsky resolves that Vergunov would owe no one else but him for the improvement of his financial prospects. Dostoevsky wanted to make sure that Vergunov would be obliged only to him for his material success.

Dostoevsky is intoxicated with romantic rhetoric. He congratulates himself on his heroic victory over the "egoism of the passions." He speaks of the sanctity of his love. But he does not always succeed in hiding from himself the morbid aspects of his adventure. "At all times here I am mad in the exact meaning of the term. . . . My spirit does not heal and will never heal." And in another letter to Wrangel he writes, "I love her insanely.... I know that in many respects I act absurdly in my relations with her, that there's almost no hope for me — but whether there may be hope or not is all the same to me. I cannot think about anyone else. To see her only, only to hear her...I am a poor madman....A love of this sort is an illness."

The passion of Dostoevsky, intensified by Maria Dmitrievna's infatuation for Vergunov, began to weaken when this infatuation diminished. Marriage then became inevitable, and, more than ever in his letters to Wrangel, Dostoevsky speaks of sacrifice, nobility, and idealism. Outwardly nothing has changed; the language remains the same but the situation has become radically transformed. The rhetoric had been just recently serving to justify an irresistible attraction, but henceforth it had to support a vacillating will:

> What a rotter I would be, think about it, if for no reason other than living a life of ease, lazy and without a care — I renounced the happiness of having for a wife the person who is dearer to me than anything in the world, if I passed by disregarding her sufferings, if I forgot her, abandoned her, solely because of a few cares that may one day disturb my so very precious existence.

Dostoevsky was a courageous man. His obsessions had not destroyed in him his will and sense of responsibility. He married Maria Dmitrievna, and Vergunov was witness. Immediately this became a catastrophe. The new husband was overwhelmed by an attack of epilepsy in the carriage that took him and his wife to Semipalatinsk. Maria Dmitri-

evna fell ill of terror. Upon arriving it was necessary for him
to prepare for a military review. Their life together began
with quarrels, money worries, apartment problems, but the
greatest unhappiness was the indifference of the husband toward his wife. This is never expressed in Dostoevsky's letters
but is easy to deduce from everything the letters say and do
not say. It was an indifference of feelings, of the heart and
spirit, an indifference that Feodor Mikhailovich doubtlessly
did his all to combat. But he never succeeded in mastering
it. This indifference had possessed him before his marriage,
from the very moment he had become certain that no one
contended with him any longer for the possession of Maria
Dmitrievna.

The presence of the rival, the fear of failure, of the
obstacle, had on Dostoevsky an influence simultaneously
paralyzing and exciting, just as on his heroes. One can confirm this once again in 1862, when he became the lover of
Pauline Suslova, the model for all the grand proud women
of the master works. At first he dominated the young
woman with all the weight of his age and celebrity. He
refused to divorce his wife for her, and his passion was
not intensified until she turned away from him and became
love-smitten, in Paris, with a Spanish medical student.

In 1859, some time after his marriage to Maria Dmitrievna, Dostoevsky had received the long solicited permission
to leave the military service, return to Russia, and, at last, to
resume his writing career. He published initially some tales
and short stories which rate among the most mediocre of
his works; then in 1861–62 *The House of the Dead* came
out, the great commentary on the Siberian prison, which
met with dazzling success, propelling its author upon the
St. Petersburg scene for the second time. In 1860 Dostoev-

sky published also a novel, *The Insulted and Injured,* to that date the most ambitious of his career.

The main character is a young writer named Vanya who experienced a rapid success followed by a period of relative oblivion, like Dostoevsky himself. Vanya is in love with Natasha, who holds him in highest esteem but does not love him. Natasha in turn loves Alyosha but hardly esteems him. Vanya does his best to facilitate the amorous relationship of Natasha and Alyosha. His attitude recalls that of Dostoevsky himself toward Vergunov and Maria Dmitrievna. All the biographies and critiques of Dostoevsky have recognized in *The Insulted and Injured* very clear allusions to the experiences in Kuznetsk. But the works prior to Siberia prefigure this experience, as we have seen. Thus *The Insulted and Injured* does not provide any really new element from the psychological point of view.

The plot of the novel would seem almost comical if one reduced it to its fundamentals. Although Natasha deserted the family household for Alyosha and so was cursed by her father, Alyosha does not love her. He loves another young woman, Katya. In short, Dostoevsky redoubles his original schema: whereas the young writer pushes Natasha into the arms of Alyosha, Natasha in turn pushes Alyosha into the arms of Katya. Katya does not want to be in debt to such grandeur of soul, so she repels Alyosha with all her might and sends him back to the unhappy Natasha.

Such are the obsessions of the work prior to prison that reappear in this novel, more pressing, more worrying, more intolerable than ever. With time the structural lines of this obsession stand out, become more definite, and simplify themselves like the features of a face in the hands of a caricaturist. In all the writings of this period Dostoevsky

multiplies the obsessional situations and marks them out
in such relief that it is nearly impossible to mistake their
character.

All the characters of *The Insulted and Injured* take
a painful pleasure, quite intense, at the spectacle of an
amorous disaster to which they contributed their best collaboration. Even before abandoning Natasha for Katya,
Alyosha was guilty of numerous infidelities with women of
low morals. He goes to see his fiancée after each of his es-
capades and gives her his story. "Upon seeing her so sweet
and mild, Alyosha could hold it in no longer and began his
confession right away without being asked to do so, solely
to relieve his heart for 'being as before,' according to his
own expression." The young woman listens to his confidences with a passionate attention: "Ah! don't get away
from your subject," she exclaims. The pleasure that Natasha takes in pardoning his indiscretions, even though she
is dreadfully jealous, reveals still more clearly the ambiguous character of the Dostoevskyan "magnanimity." "We
quarreled," she explains to Vanya, "then, when he had been
with a certain Minna...I found it out, I watched it, and —
you can imagine — I suffered terribly; and dare I admit
it? — I experienced a feeling sweet, pleasant...I don't know
why." Vanya himself, in love with Natasha, feels doubly
humiliated in his humiliation. In this scene there is a masochism and voyeurism to the second power, of which the
novel furnishes examples without number.

The dream of a life à trois is transformed into a total
nightmare. Alyosha wants to instigate a meeting between
Natasha and Katya. " 'You are created to be sisters,' " he
asserts. 'You must love each other — this is the thought that
does not leave me. I would like to see you together and to

be there so that I can gaze at you. Don't go conjecturing anything, Natasha, and let me speak of her. When I am with you, I have the desire to speak of her, and with her, to speak of you.' ... His words seem to produce on her the effect of a caress and at the same time to make her suffer."

It is clear that these love affairs are born only from the obstacle that opposes them by means of a third person, and they exist only through this third. Soon the object of rivalry appears as nothing but a simple pretext and the two rivals end up alone, face to face. The personal nullity of Alyosha, whom Natasha and Katya send back and forth to each other as they would a ball, sets in sharper relief the confrontation of the two women. Finally the two meet:

> Katya hurried forward toward Natasha, took her by the hand, and pressed her small swollen mouth upon hers. Thus entwined, they both began to cry. Katya sat on the arms of Natasha's armchair and hugged her in her arms.

Despite the flashes of brilliance that illumine it, *The Insulted and Injured* does not rank among the great works of Dostoevsky. The novel unfolds from end to end in a climate of romantic idealism which must be described as mystifying. The sentimental rhetoric places a lifestyle that depends more and more visibly on psychopathological "masochism" in a false light of moral effort and a spirit of sacrifice.

Chapter 2

Underground Psychology

In certain respects the Dostoevsky of *The Insulted and Injured* is more alienated from his own proper genius than the Dostoevsky of *The Double*. It is even this remoteness — one is tempted to say this straying — that suggests a rupture is inevitable. But only the rupture is visible at this point, and not the imminence of genius. If Dostoevsky had gone mad in 1863 rather than starting to write *Notes from the Underground,* it would have been easy to detect the foreshadowing of this madness in *The Insulted and Injured.* And perhaps there was no other outcome for the Dostoevsky of 1863 than madness or genius.

We certainly see, now, that the advance toward novelistic mastery is not a continual progress, a cumulative process, comparable to the erection of any sort of building in successive stages. *The Insulted and Injured* is certainly technically superior to the works of the beginning, for the lucidity yet to come is already present in certain passages and characters. However, this novel is still at the extreme point of blindness because of the disequilibrium with which it is affected and the divergence that is visible between the author's perspective and the objective meaning of the action. And this extreme point could only anticipate and announce either final darkness or the light of truth.

There is no task more essential, though none is more neglected, than comparing the same writer's superior works to those that are not. To facilitate this comparison we will set aside for the moment *Notes from the Underground,* a work infinitely rich and diverse, and turn to a novel six years later, *The Eternal Husband* (1870). If we digress for a moment from chronological order, this is only for practical reasons and to facilitate the understanding of our point of view. *The Eternal Husband* is exclusively devoted to obsessional motives which we emphasized in the works of the romantic period and in the Siberian correspondence. This story will thus permit us to sketch, concerning certain very specific points, an initial comparison and an initial distinction between the two Dostoevskys, the one with genius and the other without it.

The Eternal Husband is the account of Pavel Pavlovitch Trusotsky, a provincial notable who leaves for St. Petersburg after the death of his wife; his object is to find there her one-time lovers. The narrative fully illuminates the fascination exercised on Dostoevsky's heroes by the individual who humiliates them sexually. In *The Insulted and Injured* we have noted the insignificance of the lover, which would suggest the importance of rivalry in sexual passion. In *The Eternal Husband* the wife is dead, the object desired has disappeared, and the rival remains. The essential character of the obstacle is fully disclosed.

Upon his arrival in St. Petersburg Trusotsky can choose between the two lovers of his deceased wife. The first one, Velchaninov, is the narrator of the story. The second, Bagautov, took the place of Velchaninov with the unfaithful spouse, and his hold on her affections turned out to be more durable than his predecessor's. But Bagautov dies and Trusotsky, after the funeral rites which he attends in great

mourning, falls back on Velchaninov for want of someone better. In Trusotsky's eyes it is Begautov, because he
fooled and ridiculed him more thoroughly, who embodies
fully the essence of seduction and Don Juanism. It is this
essence he finds himself lacking, precisely because his wife
deceived him. So it is this essence that he seeks to appropriate in making himself the companion and emulator-rival of
his victorious opponent.

To understand this *masochism* it is necessary to forget the
medical terminology that usually obscures it in our eyes and
simply read *The Eternal Husband*. Trusotsky does not desire to be humiliated in the ordinary sense of the term. To
the contrary, humiliation constitutes an experience so terrible that it brings about fixation of "masochistic" feelings
on the person who humiliates or on those who resemble
the humiliator. Masochists cannot find their self-esteem except by a brilliant victory over the one who offended them.
But this one acquires in their eyes such fabulous dimensions
that only he appears to be uniquely capable of providing
what is sought. In masochism there is a sort of existential myopia which narrows the vision of the one offended
to a focus on the person of the offender. The latter defines not only the goal of the offended but the instruments
of his or her action. This is to say that internal contradiction, being inwardly torn and divided, is inevitable. The
one offended is condemned to wander endlessly around
the offender, reproducing the condition of the offense and
bringing about the offense once again. In the works we have
considered until now the repetitive character of the situations engenders a sort of involuntary humor. In *The Eternal
Husband* this repetitive character is emphasized; the writer
quite consciously draws comic effects from this.

In the second part of the novel Trusotsky decides to re-marry, and he tries to involve Velchaninov in the matter. He cannot hold to his own choice inasmuch as the appointed seducer has not confirmed it, in short, inasmuch as he has not desired the young woman whom Trusotsky desires himself.

So he invites Velchaninov to accompany him to the residence of the woman. Velchaninov tries to slip out of it, but he finally gives in, victim of a "bizarre attraction," writes Dostoevsky. The two men stop first at a jewelry shop, and the eternal husband asks the eternal lover to choose a gift for him which he will give to his future wife. They arrive subsequently at the young lady's place and Velchaninov falls again, irresistibly, into his role of seducer. He is pleasing and seductive and Trusotsky is not. Masochists are always fascinated artisans of their own unhappiness.

Why does he rush into his own humiliation? Because he is immensely vain and proud. This response is paradoxical only in appearance. When Trusotsky discovers that his wife prefers another man to him, the shock he experiences is dreadful because he makes it a duty to be the center and navel of the universe. The man is a former serf owner; he is rich. He lives in a world of masters and slaves and is incapable of envisaging a middle term between these two extremes; the least failure condemns him to servitude. A deceived husband, he pledges himself to being a sexual zero. After having thought of himself as someone from whom power and success naturally radiated, he now sees himself as human waste from whom impotence and ridicule inevitably ooze.

The greater the illusion of omnipotence, the easier it destroys itself. Between the Self and the Others there is always a comparison. Vanity adds its weight to the scales and inclines them toward the Self. But if the weight should be lacking, then the scales, abruptly readjusted, would lean toward the Other. The prestige with which we endow a rival who is too successful is always the measure of our vanity. We believe we hold the scepter of our pride firmly, but the slightest failure dispossesses us and it reappears, more dazzling than ever, in the hands of our rivals.

Just as Ordynov, in *The Landlady,* endeavors in vain to murder Murin, Trusotsky tries to kill Velchaninov. But more often he tries to find a *modus vivendi* with the fascinating rival. Like the hero of *A Weak Heart,* he hopes to see reflected in himself a little of that fabulous good fortune that he attributes to his conqueror. The "dream of the life à trois" reappears in a grotesque perspective.

The primary impulsion that animates Dostoevsky's heroes is thus not what the early works might seem to suggest. The reader of *The Insulted and Injured* who expects to remain faithful to the conscious intention of the writer ends up with formulas which radically contradict the latent meaning of the work. The critic George Haldas, for example, defines the common essence of all the characters as compassion, self-sacrifice, and surrender of all possessiveness. The critic well perceives that a "confused element" interferes with every passion, but it is by means of this very element, if one would believe it, that the characters finally gain victory. He sees a terrible struggle between love as passion and love as compassion, ending in the victory of compassion.

Far from disavowing the possessive aspect of every love, these characters are interested only in that. They seem to be generous *because they are not.* Why then do they manage to pass themselves off and to take themselves as the contrary of what they really are? Because pride is a blind and contradictory force which sooner or later always creates effects diametrically opposed to what it seeks. The most fanatical pride is the one most bound to humiliate itself before the other, which is to say that externally it resembles humility. At the least defeat the most extreme egoism makes voluntary slaves of us; in other words, viewed from the outside it resembles the spirit of sacrifice.

The sentimental rhetoric that triumphs in *The Insulted and Injured* does not disclose the paradox but plays the game in a manner that conceals the presence of pride. Dostoevsky's art during his great period does exactly the reverse. It chases pride and egoism from their hiding places and exposes their presence in the kind of behavior that is so strikingly like humility and altruism that it can be mistaken for them.

We do not discern the "masochism" of the characters of *The Insulted and Injured* unless we move beyond the intentions of the author toward an *objective truth* which we cannot be reproached for "projecting" on the novel since it becomes explicit in *The Eternal Husband*. In the work showing genius there is no more divergence between the author's subjective intentions and the objective meaning.

Flashes of brilliance unquestionably run through *The Insulted and Injured*. The title itself is insightful, leading many people to believe the novel, rarely read, is "Dostoevskyan" in the way that later works were to be. The idea that the behavior of the characters is rooted in pride is already expressed. "I am terrified," remarks Vanya, "because I see that they are all consumed by pride." However, this essential idea remains abstract, isolated, and submerged amid the idealist rhetoric. In *The Eternal Husband,* by contrast, we

have a nearly physical sensation of the morbid and grotesque vanity of the main character, a veritable distorting
mirror in which the dandy Velchaninov contemplates the
double of his own Don Juan-like conceit.

After *The Insulted and Injured* Dostoevsky experienced a
change in orientation both subtle and radical. This metamorphosis has intellectual consequences, but it is not the
fruit of an intellectual operation. Pride blinds intelligence.
Nor is the metamorphosis of the aesthetic sort. Pride may
assume all forms but it may equally dispense with form.
The Dostoevsky of Semipalatinsk, the Dostoevsky who was
writing Wrangel the letters that we know, was incapable of
writing *The Eternal Husband*. In spite of doubts which already assailed him, he obstinately continued to consider his
morbid pride and his obsession with humiliation in a self-
indulgent, rationalizing light. This Dostoevsky could write
only such works as *White Nights* and *The Insulted and
Injured*. It is not a matter of making Trusotsky an autobiographical character in the traditional sense of the term,
but of recognizing that this inspired creation is based on the
acute awareness of psychological mechanisms belonging to
the author himself, mechanisms whose tyranny rested precisely on the desperate effort of this same author to hide
from himself their meaning and even their presence.

❧

Behind the transformation of Dostoevsky's art there is a
veritable psychological conversion, and *Notes from the
Underground* will allow us to identify another element of it.
The hero of these memoirs is very much like Trusotsky. The
author himself emphasizes this in *The Eternal Husband*:
"Enough of underground psychology," cries out Velchani-

nov, exasperated by the ludicrous efforts of his ridiculous imitator. The *Notes* are more diffuse, less "well composed," than *The Eternal Husband,* but with a scope more vast. The "symptoms" that the underground protagonist presents are not new to us, but they are inscribed in a larger existential setting. It is not from sexual inferiority that the hero suffers but from inferiority grown rampant. His case should convince us that the morbid traits shown by Trusotsky are not of the specifically sexual type and will not be relieved by some sex-obsessed therapy in the style of Freudian psychoanalysis.

A puny and feeble creature, the underground hero belongs, unfortunately for him, to that pretentious and lamentable bureaucratic class whose mentality the writer deems extremely significant. Indeed, in some ways he views it as even prophetic of the society then in gestation.

The problem of the rival appears under a very pure, quasi-abstract form in the first "adventure" related in *Notes.* One day in a café an officer, whose way our stunted character blocks, seizes the latter by the shoulders and deposits him a little farther away, without even showing him the respect of speaking to him. The memory of this insult haunts the underground man. In his imagination the unknown officer takes on proportions as monstrous as Velchaninov in Trusotsky's fantasies.

Every obstacle, every appearance of an obstacle, sets in motion psychological mechanisms already observed in *The Eternal Husband.* A second adventure occurs to confirm this point. The former schoolmates of the underground man hold a party. The underground man deems himself quite superior to them and as usual does not desire to be with them, but the feeling of being excluded from the celebration awak-

ens in him a frantic need to be invited. The contempt he
believes himself to inspire in these mediocre persons confers
on them a prodigious importance.

The idea that pride is the origin of the imaginary grandeur and actual baseness of the underground character is
more developed than in *The Eternal Husband*. In his solitary dreams the hero elevates himself effortlessly up to the
seventh heaven; no obstacle stops him. But a moment always arrives when the dream no longer suffices for him.
Egotistic exaltation has nothing to do with the Buddhist
nirvana. Sooner or later it must prove itself in reality. The
solitary dream is always a fantasy of the arms of the knight
errant. But the dream is frenzied and its realization is impossible. The underground man throws himself therefore
into humiliating adventures, and he falls as deeply down in
reality as he ascended to the heights in his dream.

The morals that are based on harmony between the general interest and private interests "properly understood,"
confuse pride with egoism in a traditional sense of the term.
Their inventors do not suspect that pride is essentially contradictory, self-divided and torn between the Self and the
Other. They do not perceive that extreme egoism leads always to that extreme altruism which takes the form of
masochism and sadism. They make of pride the contrary of
what it is; they make of it a power of uniting rather than
a power of dividing and dispersing. The illusion present in
the forms of individualistic thought is apparently not accidental, for it is this illusion and it alone that defines pride
correctly by virtue of its very individualism. So it is pride
itself which generates the morality of harmony between the
diverse egoisms. Indeed, the proud wish to be accused of
egoism and gladly accuse themselves of it in order bet-

ter to dissimulate the role that the Other plays in their existence.

The second part of *Notes from the Underground* reveals in striking fashion the vanity of utilitarian reasoning. The underground hero is perfectly capable of recognizing his interest "properly understood" but he has no desire to make his conduct conform to it. This interest appears terribly dull and boring beside the chimeras haunting his loneliness and the hatreds out of which his entire social existence is woven. What does our "interest" weigh, however "properly understood" it may be, beside this omnipotence of which the Other, the fascinating executioner, appears to be the possessor? The proud always finally prefer the most abject slavery to the egoism recommended by the false wisdom of a decadent humanism.

Utilitarian reasoning seems irrefutable due to its cynicism. It is no longer a matter of combatting (impossible task!) but of utilizing the irrepressible desire of individuals to reduce everything to themselves. But the cynicism is only apparent. Utilitarianism eliminates from idealism what remains in it of authentic grandeur, but it maintains and even reinforces its naiveté. Dostoevsky senses all this well: he understands that the underground discovery deals a fatal blow to the utopia of the "Crystal Palace,"* for it reveals the nothingness of the metaphysical and moral vision upon which the utopia claims to be founded. The victory — the first — over the dismal moral platitudes of the nineteenth century seems so important to him that he would like to formulate it in didactic and philosophical terms. Thus at the beginning of

---

*The Crystal Palace in London is satirized by Dostoevsky in *Notes from the Underground* as a metaphor for the blind pretensions of utilitarian technology and rationalism. — *Tr.*

his novel he charges his hero directly to refute the ethical systems whose ineptitude the narrative sequence will demonstrate. It is only this narrative sequence that is properly novelistic.

But Dostoevsky did not succeed in translating the underground psychology into concepts. Why would he read his own text better than most of his critics? He certainly saw that the underground protagonist was always choosing something other than his true interest "properly understood," but he did not know how to express what he chose or why he chose it. He lets the main point slip away. To the morality of self-interest "properly understood" he opposes hardly more than an empty and abstract freedom, a sort of "right to caprice" which really does not refute anything at all. This first part is therefore very inferior to what follows. But it is upon this part, sadly, that the critics base their argument when they seek to define Dostoevsky's anti-determinism and anti-psychologism, and it is apparently from it that Gide borrowed his famous theory of "the gratuitous act."

The text does scarcely anything more than reject, in the name of a vague irrationalism situated even lower than utilitarianism in the hierarchy of Western thought, all the positive elements that utilitarianism harbors. So in spite of its author it takes a course in the direction of new divisions and new dispersions — that is, it situates itself objectively in the trajectory of Promethean pride. It finally contradicts the novelistic part for which it intends to be the commentary. So we should not be surprised to see this text constantly cited in our time by an anarchic individualism which cannot lay claim to Dostoevsky except by leaving the best of his work to one side.

It is regrettable that some critics, hostile in principle to this anarchic individualism, themselves make much of this untypical text and seek therein Dostoevsky's understanding of freedom. These critics fall back necessarily into the perpetual division between the thinker and the novelist, a division which is established always to the detriment of the second Dostoevsky, i.e., the only one who truly counts. It is not the disincarnate thought that interests us but the thought embodied in the novels. In short, it is necessary to collaborate in the work of deciphering undertaken by the writer and not to profit from his indulgences or speculate about his weaknesses. Interpretation must not rest on the most limited aspects of the novelist's works, which are more under the sway of the past, but on what opens itself to the future and bears within it the greatest richness.

Dostoevsky the genius is Dostoevsky the novelist. The question of the meaning of freedom should therefore not be posed to his theoretical reflections but to those of his texts that are authentically and clearly novelistic. This freedom is just as radical as that of Sartre, for Dostoevsky's universe is just as void of objective values as Sartre's. But the mature and older Dostoevsky perceives, initially only at the level of novelistic creation, then also at the level of religious meditation, something that neither Sartre the novelist nor Sartre the philosopher ever perceived: in such a universe the essential choice must bear not on a mute *en soi* (in oneself), but on a mode of conduct already laden with meaning and productive of meaning whose initial model is furnished for us by others. The best child psychologies confirm the primary data of the novelistic work. In the universe structured by the Gospel revelation, individual existence remains basically imitative even, and above all, perhaps, when one rejects with horror any thought of imitation. The church fathers held as evident a truth which later became obscured and which the novelist regains step by step as he passes through the terrible consequences of this obscuration.

In the period of *Notes from the Underground* the novelist possessed the truth sufficiently to render it operative in his work, but he was no more capable than other thinkers of his era of disengaging its formulation. Thus the gratuitous, arbitrary, and brutal character of his nonfiction prose. He knows well where he finally wants to get — or at least he believes that he knows it, for there again, he may deceive himself. But he is never able logically to justify his conclusion.

Underground pride, strange thing that it is, is banal pride. The most intense suffering proceeds from the fact that the speaker does not succeed in *distinguishing himself* concretely from the persons around him. Yet he becomes aware of this failure little by little. He perceives that he is surrounded by minor bureaucrats who have the same desires and suffer the same failures as he. All underground individuals believe they are all the more "unique" to the extent that they are, in fact, alike. The mechanism of this illusion is not difficult to uncover. We have already seen that Velchaninov in *The Eternal Husband* enters in spite of himself into the game of his partner. The masochist always ends up encountering a sadist and the sadist a masochist. Each confirms for the other and for himself the double illusion of grandeur and baseness; each supports and precipitates in the other one the coming and going between exaltation and despair. Hateful imitation is further extended and sterile conflicts provoke others. Everyone cries out, with the underground character, "I'm all by myself and *they* are everyone."

Beyond superficial disagreement there is a profound agreement between social reality and individual psychology. *The Double* offered already a mixture of psychopathological fantasy and everyday reality which presupposes this agreement. The most significant scenes are those where Golyadkin Junior, the double, resorts to little ruses, ones quite classic, to supplant his rival with the department head. The rivalry of the two Golyadkins is realized in very significant situations from a sociological standpoint. To comprehend the obsessions of Dostoevsky's minor functionaries one must imagine the Czarist bureaucracy in the middle of the nineteenth century, with its extremely strict hierarchy and multiplication of useless and poorly paying jobs. The process of "depersonalization" undergone by the mass of subordinate officials becomes all the more rapid, effective, and underhanded as it becomes confused with the fierce but sterile rivalries engendered by the system. The individuals constantly opposed to one another cannot understand that their actual personalities are in the process of dissolving.

Otto Rank, in his essay on the theme of the double in literature, rightly saw that Dostoevsky was able to give a masterful and complete description of a paranoid state. This description includes the behavior of the other characters in relation to the victim's madness. Rank does not specify, unfortunately, in what this action consists. It is not enough to say that the milieu *favors* madness, for it is impossible to distinguish the two. The bureaucratic aspect is the external face of a structure whose internal face is the hallucination of the double. The phenomenon itself is double in that it bears with it a subjective dimension and an objective dimension that converge in the same result.

To be convinced of this fact, it is necessary initially to recognize that *The Double* and *Notes from the Underground* are two efforts to express the same truth. The major scenes of the two works all unfold through evenings in the fall or winter's end; a snow falls that is half melted; the characters are too cold and too hot at the same time; the weather is humid, unhealthy, ambiguous — *double,* to say it all. In the two novels we find the same types of rivalry and the same themes, including the refused invitation and the physical expulsion, which will reappear with Samuel Beckett.

If the two novels form a unity, it is finally from pride that Golyadkin's hallucination must stem. This proud man believes he is *one* in his solitary dream, but in failure he divides in two and becomes a contemptible person and a contemptuous observer of the human scene. He becomes Other to himself. The failure constrains him to take up against himself the part of this Other who reveals to him his own nothingness. Relations with himself and with others are thus characterized by a double ambivalence:

> Naturally I detested all the employees of our chancellory, from the first one to the last, and I scorned them every one; but at the same time I feared them, I believe. It even occurred to me to place them above me. With me this sort of thing always happens suddenly — now I have contempt for people and now I put them on a pedestal. An honorable and cultivated man cannot be vain except on condition of being quite demanding on himself and despising himself sometimes to the point of hatred.

Failure produces a double movement. The scornful observer, the Other who is in the Self, unceasingly approaches the Other who is outside of the Self, the triumphant rival. We have seen, moreover, that this triumphant rival, this Other outside of the Self whose desire I imitate and who imitates mine, constantly comes closer to the Self. To the extent that the interior rupture of consciousness is reenforced, the distinction between the Self and the Other weakens. The two movements converge to produce the "hallucination" of the double. The obstacle, as a corner imbedded in consciousness, aggravates the doubling or dividing effects of all reflection. The hallucinatory phenomenon constitutes the outcome and synthesis of all the subjective and objective doublings that define underground existence.

It is the mixing of subjective and objective that the story of 1846 makes us feel so marvelously. Psychiatry is incapable of correctly posing the problem of the double, for it cannot place social structures in question. It seeks to heal patients by leading them back to a "sense of objectivity." But the "objectivity" of Golyadkin is, in certain respects, superior to that of the "normal" persons surrounding him. He could utter the boastings of the underground man: "As for me, I have never done anything but push to extremes in my life what you yourselves would dare to push only halfway; in the process you call your cowardice wisdom and so console yourselves with lies. So that I am perhaps more alive than you."

So what is this thing that the underground man believes he alone "pushes to extremes" but that he shares with all his neighbors? It is evidently pride, the primary psychological (and before long metaphysical) motor which governs all the individual and collective manifestations of the underground life. If *The Double* is a remarkable work, it still does not uncover what is essential. In particular it does not reveal the role that *literature* plays in underground egotism. The *Notes* devote some fine pages to this theme. The protagonist informs us that he has cultivated "the beautiful and the sublime" all his life. He passionately admires the great romantic writers. But it is a poisonous balm that these exceptional beings pour on his psychological wounds. The great lyrical impulses divert one from what is real without truly liberating, for the ambitions they awake are, after all, terribly mundane. The victim of romanticism always becomes more and more unfit for life, while demanding of it things more and more excessive. Literary individualism is a sort of drug whose doses must be ceaselessly augmented in order to procure a few doubtful raptures at the price of sufferings which continually increase. The separation between the "ideal" and sordid reality is increased. After having played the angel, the underground hero plays the beast. The doublings multiply.

In this respect Dostoevsky satirizes his own romanticism. The contrast between lamentable situations and grandiose rhetoric, both so intoxicating to the underground hero, corresponds to the gap between the interpretation suggested by the author and the objective meaning of a novel such as *The Insulted and Injured*. The underground character perceives the truth of the grotesque adventures he has lived in blindness. This divergence between the person he has become and the person he was before reflects the difference that separates *Notes* from the prior works, which we will henceforth call "romantic."

Romantics never recognize their own doublings, and thus they only make them worse. Romantics want to believe they are perfectly *one*. They choose one of the two halves of themselves — in the romantic era properly named, this is

generally the ideal and sublime half, while in our day it is
rather the sordid half. But whichever half, the romantic tries
to pass it off as the totality. Pride seeks to prove that it can
gather and unify everything real around itself.

For the romantic Dostoevsky the two halves of romantic consciousness are reflected separately in the sentimental
or pathetic works on the one hand, and in the grotesque
works on the other. On one side there are *Poor Folk, The
Landlady, White Nights,* and on the other *Mr. Prokharchin,
The Village of Stepanchikova, The Dream of the Uncle,* etc.
In works such as *The Insulted and Injured* the division of
persons into "good" and "bad" reflects the underground
duality. This subjective duality is presented to us as an objective datum of what is real. The difference between "the
good" and "the bad" is just as radical as it is abstract;
the elements are the same in the two instances, though expressed with a little more adequacy or a little less in given
instances. Theoretically no communication is possible between the two halves, but the masochism of the "good"
and the sadism of the "bad" reveal the instability of the
structure, the perpetual tendency of the two halves to pass
into one another without ever achieving a complete merger.
Masochism and sadism mirror the romantic nostalgia for
lost unity, but this nostalgia is mingled with pride. Far from
reintegrating, the desire it produces rather disperses, for it
wanders always toward the Other.

So the romantic work cannot rescue the author, for it
encloses him in the circle of his pride and perpetuates the
mechanism of an existence destined for failure and fascination. In *Notes* Dostoevsky alludes to the self-divided art he
is in the process of renouncing when he describes for us the
feeble literary attempts of his hero. The impotent desire to

avenge oneself pushes the latter not to satirize himself, but to satirize his rival, the enemy, the arrogant officer: "One fine morning, although I had never occupied myself with literature, it popped into my mind to describe this officer in a satirical tone, to caricature him and make him the hero of a story. I plunged myself happily into this work. I depicted my hero in the most dismal colors, I even slandered him."

All the works of the romantic period, with the partial exception of *The Double,* do nothing other than reflect a duality that the works of genius reveal. The underground character is *simultaneously* the "dreaming" and lyrical hero of the sentimental works and the minor bureaucrat, scheming and ridiculous, of the grotesque works. The two halves of underground consciousness have been rejoined. It is not their impossible synthesis that the writer presents but their painful juxtaposition in the heart of the same individual. The two halves alternately dominate the personality of the unfortunate hero. The work that reveals the division is a work that *gathers.*

శ

We have no difficulty locating in the existence of Dostoevsky himself the painful duality that characterizes underground existence. The personal memories that the writer utilizes in *Notes* polarize, apparently, around the later years of his adolescence.

The childhood of Feodor Mikhailovich unfolded in the shadow of a father as sometimes capricious in his conduct as he was always austere in his principles. Literature thus became a means of fleeing the sad realities of family life. This tendency toward "evasion" was subsequently reenforced by the young Shidlovsky, who became a close

friend of the two Dostoevsky brothers on the very day of
their arrival in St. Petersburg, in 1837. Shidlovsky swore
only by Corneille, Rousseau, Schiller, and Victor Hugo. He
wrote verses in which he expressed a need to "govern the
universe" and to "converse with God." He cried a lot; he
spoke even of making an end to his wretched existence
by throwing himself into a canal of St. Petersburg. Feodor
Mikhailovich was subjugated: he admired what Shidlovsky
admired; he thought what Shidlovsky thought. It seems that
his writer's vocation dates from this period.

Some months later, Dostoevsky entered the sinister School
of Military Engineers of St. Petersburg. The discipline was
ferocious, the studies unproductive and distressing. Dostoevsky was suffocating in the milieu of young dullards
completely occupied with their career and their social life.
If the solitary dreams of the underground character recall
Shidlovsky, the misadventures that follow them make us
think of the School of Engineers. After having long hidden
from himself the sufferings to which his fellow students sub-
jected him, Dostoevsky perhaps exaggerates them a little.
Strong enough, thereafter, to face his weaknesses directly,
he is still too weak to pardon the offenders.

It was during these school years that Dostoevsky's father
was murdered by serfs over whom he tyrannized as he did
his children.* In the grip of the idea that he feels com-

---

*Since the original publication of this monograph, research in local archives
has cast doubt on whether an actual murder occurred. Joseph Frank points
out that the death was investigated by local authorities, "and that two
doctors had certified the cause as being the apoplexy from which Dr. Dostoevsky had long suffered. A neighbor, who wished to purchase the property,
spread the rumor of the murder, and this was presumably accepted by
the absent Dostoevsky family" (Frank, *Through the Russian Prism: Essays
on Literature and Culture* [Princeton: Princeton University Press, 1990],
113 n. 8). Of course, whether a fact or not, Dostoevsky's belief that his

forted by the father's death and that he is, therefore, even
an accomplice in it, Feodor Mikhailovich experiences an extreme anxiety and he does his utmost to expel the horrible
recollection from his memory.

Just out of the military academy, Dostoevsky writes *Poor
Folk* and is hailed as a new Gogol in the circle of Belinsky's
friends. He goes from poverty to luxury, from anonymity to
renown, from obscurity to the public spotlight. The most
delirious dreams of Shidlovsky become reality. Dostoevsky is drunk with joy. His pride, crushed but still alive,
rises again and blooms. He writes to Michael, "Never, my
brother, will my glory surpass the summit which it has now
attained. Everywhere I excite incredible respect, an amazing
curiosity.... Everyone considers me a wonder." The report
spreads, he states with satisfaction, "that a new star has just
appeared and will push everyone else into the mud."

The young writer takes all the flattery quite seriously. He
does not understand that this is a short-term loan, and that
he must pay back everything right away, under penalty of
losing his credit. Dostoevsky does not practice any of the
little compromises that make the literary underground tol-
erable. His pride is no doubt greater than that of the people
around him, but he is too naive, too crude, less able to spare
the pride of others. This young provincial, boiling with un-
sated desires, yet already mistreated by life to the point of
remaining forever deformed, could not avoid at once amus-
ing and irritating the literary dandies who gathered around
Ivan Turgenev, one of the members of the Belinsky circle
who was to be a dominant figure in Russian literature.

Dostoevsky had long chosen to be god, far from people

father was murdered would accordingly affect his emotional life and creative
work. — *Tr.*

and society. Here he is now, entering as an acclaimed figure into the most brilliant literary salons of St. Petersburg. It is thus no surprise that he takes himself for a god. Contemporary sources all describe his astonishing transformation. At first extremely quiet and self-contained, he subsequently demonstrated extraordinary exuberance and arrogance. The others initially smiled at this, but soon they were annoyed.

All the underground mechanisms then began to function. Their pride injured, Turgenev and his friends attempt to injure in turn. Dostoevsky tries to defend himself, but the match is not equal. He accused Turgenev, whom he had until then venerated, of being "jealous" of his work. He lets it be known that his giant's wings prevent him from merely walking (from Baudelaire in *Les fleurs du mal*). The mockers break loose and satirical verses, the work of Turgenev and Nekrasov, start to circulate. In a satirical poem called "The Knight of the Rueful Countenance," Dostoevsky is labeled a "pimple" on the face of Russian literature, is mocked for his inflated opinion of his literary creativity, and ridiculed for fainting when he was introduced to a beautiful belle of the aristocracy who wanted to meet him.*

The superficial Panaev would note a little later in his *Recollections,* "We made one of the little idols of the day lose his head....He had finished by rambling. Soon we unhinged him and forgot him. Poor wretch! We ridiculed him."

Here we see the closing of the circle of pride and humiliation. Nothing more banal, in a sense, than this circle, but Dostoevsky is not yet capable of describing it, for he has not yet begun to extricate himself from it. Dostoevsky is certainly proud *in his own way,* and this way is unique. This

---

*Joseph Frank, *Dostoevsky: The Seeds of Revolt* (Princeton: Princeton University Press, 1976), 168.

singularity is not without importance, since it is reflected in his work, but it is less important for this work than the common features between Dostoevsky and the rest of the human race. If his pride was not made from the same stuff as the pride of others, critics could not reproach the writer, as they often do, for being *more* proud, and also *more* humiliated, than the common run of mortals. This *more* of pride is mysteriously tied to the *less* that will permit Dostoevsky a little later to recognize in himself and analyze the underground mechanisms. This *more* and this *less* instruct us better concerning the genesis of novelistic genius than the ineffable singularity seen by so many of the critics. We must always return to the sentence from the *Notes* cited above: "As for me, I have never done anything but push to extremes in my life what you yourselves would dare to push only halfway...."

If the dialectic of pride and humiliation were not as dominant as the inspired Dostoevsky would affirm, we could understand neither the success of the many novelists who conceal it nor the genius of the writer who reveals to us its universality. Nor would we be able to understand the delayed blossoming of this genius for we would not be able to comprehend the relations of Dostoevsky with Belinsky and his friends. Dostoevsky had worked on *The Double* in a state of exaltation easy to understand. In giving a realistic and everyday dimension to a romantic theme repeated over and over again, the writer was carrying his work toward unexplored depths. His joy is perhaps comparable to that of the scientific investigator who combines luck with ability and discovers all at once the solution to a problem which might have required of him numerous groping attempts. The motif of the double permits Dostoevsky to penetrate into a literary domain to which he was still incapable of gaining access by his own powers. Perhaps he would have never fully conquered and possessed this domain if his work had been welcomed on its actual merits. Indeed, perhaps he would have yielded to the temptation to repeat the success of *the Double* and to congeal the technique of this novel, so particular to it, into a permanent method. Such a Dostoevsky would be more purely "literary" than the real Dostoevsky, more "modern" and "postmodern" perhaps, in the sense that many people today give this term; but he would be less universal and finally less great.

So it could be that when Belinsky, with some hesitations, condemned *The Double*, he rendered a great service to his protégé, but for reasons quite different from those that he imagined. Dostoevsky was now exasperating him, and he himself was too egotistical, too much a man of letters, not to indulge himself in going on to play the sadistic role that the young writer's masochism invited. Aside from the question of the borrowings from Gogol, the objections the critic made to *The Double* were very simplistic. But how could Dostoevsky question the judgment of the person who had wrenched him away from his horrible adolescence? The letters he wrote to his brother reveal a great confusion. "I was momentarily discouraged. I have a terrible fault: a pride, a vanity without limits. The thought alone of having disappointed the public's expectation and bungled a literary work which could be quite impressive literally kills me. Golyadkin disgusts me. Quite a few passages were patched together. All this makes life unbearable for me."

Just as Velchaninov finally enters into the game of Trusotsky, Belinsky and his friends act as *doubles* and tighten the circle of failure around Dostoevsky. They close off to

him what would have been an honorable career, even brilliant, in literature. They help him to suffocate in embryo the
writer of talent he could have been. The works after *The
Double* justify, by their mediocrity, the condemnation without appeal that Belinsky brought against them. Only two
paths remain open to Dostoevsky: complete alienation or
genius. His actual course was initially the way of alienation
and subsequently the way of genius.

Chapter 3

Underground Metaphysics

After *Notes from the Underground,* Dostoevsky composed *Crime and Punishment,* the work that was for a long time, and perhaps remains yet, his most celebrated. Raskolnikov is a solitary dreamer, subject to alternations of exaltation and depression. He is obsessed with the fear of being ridiculed. He is thus an underground person, but he is more tragic than grotesque because he tries fiercely to test and surpass the invisible limits of his prison. The need for action, which for his underground predecessor was realized only in feeble and sorry gestures, leads this time to an atrocious crime. Raskolnikov kills, and he kills deliberately in order to place his pride on an unshakable foundation. The underground hero reigns over his individual universe, but his royalty is threatened each instant by the invasion of others. Raskolnikov imagines that his crime, in excluding him from the morality of the human community, will avoid this danger.

It is true that his crime isolates Raskolnikov more radically than his dreaming did. But the meaning of this isolation, which the hero had hitherto believed to be determined by his own will, is always in question. Raskolnikov does not know whether his solitude makes him superior or inferior to other humans, an individual god or an individual earthworm. And the Other remains the arbiter of this debate.

Raskolnikov, after all, is not less fascinated by the judges than Trusotsky by his Don Juan model or the underground character by his officer bullies. Raskolnikov depends, in and for his being, on the verdict of the Other.

The detective mystery transforms the underground hero into an actual suspect, under surveillance by real police agents, and brought before real judges who will judge him in an actual tribunal. In making his hero commit an actual crime, Dostoevsky magisterially throws into relief this most extreme self-division. Even the name of the main character suggests this duality. *Raskol* means schism, separation. The writers of the twentieth century will unceasingly take up this mythic incarnation of underground psychology, but they will sometimes correct it in an individualistic direction: they will give it the conclusion that Raskolnikov tries in vain to make come true. One cannot read these works without wondering why the motif of the trial exercises such fascination on their authors. The conclusion would perhaps be less simple and less reassuring if this very fascination, rather than the "innocence" of the hero and the "injustice" of the society, had become a subject for reflection.

The reverie of Raskolnikov is just as literary as that of the underground man, but it is differently oriented. For the romantic "beautiful and sublime" is substituted the figure of Napoleon, the quasi-legendary model of all the great ambitious figures of the nineteenth century. The Napoleon of Raskolnikov is more "Promethean" than romantic. The superior humanity that he embodies is the fruit of a more extreme pride, but the fundamental project has not changed. And Raskolnikov cannot escape from the underground oscillations; he succeeds only in giving them a terrible intensity. In other words, this *more* of pride does not succeed in enabling Raskolnikov to emerge from the underground.

In *Thus Spoke Zarathustra* Nietzsche would certainly ascribe the failure of Raskolnikov to the cowardice of the "last man," that is, to underground cowardice. Like Dostoevsky, Nietzsche believes he recognizes in what takes place around him a *passion* of modern pride. We can understand his emotion when the accident of browsing in a bookstore front brought into his hands a copy of *Notes from the Underground.* He recognized there a masterful depiction of what he himself called *ressentiment.* It is the same problem, and Dostoevsky poses it almost in the same way. The response of Dostoevsky is different, no doubt, but *Crime and Punishment,* in spite of Sonya and the Christian conclusion, still remains quite distant from final certainty. For yet some time Dostoevsky would ask himself whether a pride even more extreme than that of Raskolnikov could not succeed where this hero had failed.

&

After *Crime and Punishment* came *The Gambler* (1867). The hero is a *utchitel* — a tutor — in the home of a Russian general who is stationed, with his family, at a German post. He experiences an underground passion for the general's daughter, Pauline, who treats him with a contemptuous indifference. It is his awareness of being regarded as *nothing* that renders her as *everything* in the eyes of this new underground character. In her the goal and the obstacle merge, the desired object and the haunting rival become one. "I have the impression," remarks the *utchitel,* "that she has regarded me like that empress of ancient times who undressed before her slave, not considering him to be a man. Yes, she doesn't even consider me a man."

Behind the untouchableness of Pauline the *utchitel* imagines an utterly complete pride which he seeks desperately to grasp and assimilate to himself. But the situation is turned around one evening when Pauline comes to the young man's room and quite simply offers herself to him. Away then with the attitude of servility! The *utchitel* abandons Pauline and rushes to the casino, where he wins in one night a fortune at roulette. The next morning he does not even try to rejoin his beloved. A French prostitute, who had formerly annoyed him unmercifully, takes him off to Paris and spends all his money. It is enough that Pauline is revealed to be vulnerable for her to lose her prestige in the eyes of the *utchitel*. The empress becomes the slave and he the master. This is why the *utchitel*, who was awaiting the "favorable moment," decided to gamble. Here we are in a world where there are only underground relationships, even with roulette. Having treated Pauline with the casual firmness suited to masters, he is certain it will be the same from now on with the game of roulette, and victory on both fronts is assured.

The game of love becomes the same thing as the game of chance. In the underground world the Other exercises a force of gravitation that one cannot conquer except in opposing it with a pride denser and heavier, around which this very Other will be constrained to gravitate. But in itself pride weighs nothing for it *is* not; it does not acquire density and weight, in fact, except through the homage of the Other. Mastery and slavery therefore depend on infinitesimal details the same as in roulette, in which the stopping of the marble on this or that number depends on causes that are minuscule and incalculable. The lover is thus delivered over to the same chance as the gambler. In the domain of human relations, however, one may remove oneself from chance by dissimulating one's desire. To dissimulate one's desire is to present to the Other an image, necessarily deceptive, of a satisfied pride; it is to compel the Other to reveal his own desire and to compel him thereby to despoil himself of all prestige. But to dissimulate one's desire it is necessary to be perfectly the master of oneself. The mastery of self permits the domination of underground chance. Starting from that point, to believe that chance, in every area of existence, is subject to individuals who sufficiently master themselves, it requires only one step, and it is this step the *utchitel* takes in *The Gambler.* The entire story rests on the secret identity between eroticism and gambling. "Very often," remarks the *utchitel,* "women are lucky in gambling; they have an extraordinary mastery of themselves."

Roulette, like the apparently untouchable female, mistreats those who let themselves be fascinated by her, those whose fear of losing is too great. It loves only the fortunate. The gambler who becomes obsessive, like the unfortunate lover, never succeeds in climbing the fatal slope. This is certainly why the rich alone win, for they can treat themselves to the luxury of losing. Money attracts money, as likewise only the Don Juans seduce women because they deceive them all. The laws of the capitalist free market, like those of eroticism, stem from underground pride.

During this entire period Dostoevsky, as his correspondence shows, is really persuaded that a little composure would permit him to win at roulette. But he is never able to apply his "method," for, upon the first gains or losses, he becomes caught up in emotion and falls once more into slavery. He loses, in short, because he is too vulnerable, psychologically and financially. With him the passion for gambling is confused with the illusion produced by underground pride. This illusion consists in extending to the domain of physical nature the influence that the mastery of self exercises over the underground world. The illusion does not consist in believing that one is god, but that one can make oneself divine. It does not have an intellectual character, but is so deeply rooted that Dostoevsky will not succeed in wrenching himself away from the gambling tables until 1871.

To grasp the relation between eroticism and money we must juxtapose to *The Gambler* the scene in *The Idiot* where Nastasya Filippovna throws a packet of banknotes into the fire. The young woman is ready contemptuously to throw over the man who will make the least gesture toward this money that is burning up. The woman is substituted for roulette, whereas in the principal scene of *The Gambler* it is roulette that is substituted for the woman. In any case, it matters little to distinguish too neatly between these two ordeals of underground pride, eroticism and gambling.

Money has always played an important role in underground fantasy. Mr. Prokharchin, the hero of a story immediately following *The Double,* is a solitary old man who lives and dies like a beggar beside his money. One of the observers of this lamentable existence wonders whether the unhappy fellow dreams of being Napoleon. This avaricious character is a precursor of Raskolnikov.

The theme of money in the service of the will to power reappears in *A Raw Youth* (1874), Dostoevsky's penultimate novel. The hero Arkady dreams not of being Napoleon, but Rothschild. Money, he speculates, offers mediocre persons in the modern world a way of lifting themselves

above other people. It is not that Arkady ascribes any concrete value to wealth; he simply wants to obtain it in order
to throw it at the heads of the *others*. The Rothschild fantasy, like the Napoleon fantasy, stems from the fascination
that the Other holds over underground pride.

This fantasy, which is simultaneously grandiose and mea-
ger, belongs to the moment of egotistic exaltation: the I
pretends to extend its conquests over the totality of being.
But a single look from the Other is enough to disperse these
riches. Then it is a veritable bankruptcy, financially and
spiritually, which becomes actual through excessive expen-
ditures followed by humiliating loans. The fantasy remains,
but it passes on to a second state. Arkady dresses like a
prince and leads the life of a dandy.

For Dostoevsky's characters prodigality is quite frequent,
in all the periods of his career. But we must wait until *A
Raw Youth* to encounter it united with avarice. Formerly,
the misers were nothing but misers and the prodigals were
nothing but prodigals. The classic tradition of *character*
remained more strongly in place. It is, however, the juxtaposition of contraries, i.e., union without reconciliation, that
defines the underground in all its aspects. It is this "broad-
ness" that, in Dostoevsky's eyes, defines the Russian and
perhaps the modern human being in general. It is in the passion for gambling—miserly prodigality, wasteful avarice—
that this union of contraries is revealed. In roulette the
moments of the dialectic succeed each other very quickly
and cease to be distinct. At each spin mastery and slavery
are at stake. Roulette is the abstract quintessence of alter-
ity in a universe where all human relations are affected by
underground pride.

Dostoevsky the genius unites, as we have already said, elements of underground psychology that remain isolated and divided in the prior works. It is this creative process that we find, once again, in the character of Arkady. Dostoevsky understands in *A Raw Youth,* better than in *The Gambler,* the role that money played in his own life. This perception desacralizes money and makes underground fetishism recede. Until about 1870, most of the novelist's letters may be grouped in two categories: those that are full of sensational projects which are bound to assure a life of ease for their author and his kin; the others are requests for money, frantic or imploring. In 1871 at Wiesbaden Dostoevsky again suffers heavy losses at the game tables. And he announces to his wife, once again, that he is healed of his passion. But this time he speaks true. Never again does he set foot in a gambling casino.

ɚ

Is it possible to escape from the underground by mastering oneself? This question is connected to the question of Raskolnikov, the question of Nietzsche's Overman. It is at the center of *The Idiot* and *Demons,* the two masterwork novels that follow *The Gambler.* Both were composed while he and his family were in self-imposed exile. They sojourned in Germany and Italy from 1867 to 1871.

For Prince Myshkin the mastery of self does not stem in principle from pride but from humility. The original idea of the prince is that of the perfect human. The substance of his being, the essence of his personality, is clearly humility, while pride, by contrast, defines the very basis, the essence of the underground personality. Around Myshkin we find otherwise the teeming underground agitation of the preceding works.

The primary model for Myshkin is a Christ more romantic than Christian, that of Jean-Paul, of Vigny, of Nerval in *The Chimères,* a Christ always isolated from human beings and from his Father in a perpetual and somewhat theatrical agony. This Christ "sublime" and "ideal" is also a Christ impotent to redeem humankind, a Christ who dies without resurrection. Myshkin's anxiety before the too realistic *Descent from the Cross* by Holbein symbolizes the dissociation of flesh and spirit to which romantic idealism leads.

The weaknesses of the model reappear in the disciple. The somewhat caricatured humility of Myshkin is initially conceived as perfection, but as one proceeds through the novel it appears more and more to be a kind of infirmity, a diminution of existence, a veritable deficiency of being. We finally see the reappearance of the self-divisions, unquestionable symptoms of underground masochism. Myshkin is divided in his emotional life. He abandons Aglaya for the sake of the unfortunate Nastasya Filippovna, who inspires in him an obsessive "pity" rather than love. The prince and Rogozhin are *doubles* of one another, that is, the two halves, forever disjointed and mutilated, of underground consciousness.

The conclusion, which is exceptionally powerful, shows us these two "halves" together beside the corpse of Nastasya Filippovna. The two "halves" are both disclosed to be incapable, the one as much as the other, of saving the poor wretched woman. Rogozhin is bestial sensuality, always underlying disincarnate idealism. It is thus necessary to recognize in the final catastrophe the consequence of the romantic inability to embody itself. The entire spiritual life of Myshkin, which is tied to epilepsy and his passion for humility, may be only the supreme form of that voluptuousness which makes the inhabitants of the underground relish humiliation.

The Idiot, the novel that Dostoevsky had wanted to be so luminous, turns out to be the darkest of all, the only one that ends on a note of despair. A supreme effort to create a purely human and individualist perfection, the novel turns back against its own "idea." In it we encounter again, but at a superior level, the conclusions of *Notes from the Underground*. The failure of the initial idea is the triumph of another idea, more profound, one of despair only because it does not yet appear in its own fullness. Such a failure could not be deduced from a mediocre work, so it implies the most brilliant literary success. *The Idiot* is one of the summits of Dostoevsky's work. Its "experimental" character confers on it an existential depth with which very few works are endowed.

The second model of Myshkin is a Don Quixote revised and corrected by romanticism, i.e., once again an "idealist" and pathetic victim of his own perfection. This Don Quixote is not the one created by Cervantes, just as the Myshkin copied after him is not the "true" Myshkin. It is in the failure of the idea of perfection that Dostoevsky becomes, without a doubt, the equal of Cervantes. Behind the romantic pseudo-perfection the same demons always reappear. The popular view of *The Idiot* suppresses the demons and falls into affectedness. Dostoevsky finally rejected the idea that all the Myshkins of the cinema convey to us, eyed and fussed over by beautiful ladies in crinoline. These interpretations of Myshkin are always extraordinarily "spiritual," with their long-suffering melancholy and the eternal beard that surrounds the face and conceals half of it.

&

What is the source of the misunderstanding between Myshkin and the Others? Is it necessary to cast all the blame
on the Others? The consequences, almost infallibly disas-
trous, of Myshkin's interventions require us to pose the
question. When General Ivolgin launches out with his boastings, Lebedyev and his companions in drinking bouts do not
hesitate to interrupt him, and this forces the old buffoon not
to go beyond certain limits. But Myshkin does not interrupt
him; and the general pushes his frenzy of braggadocio so
far that he can no longer believe his own lies. Overwhelmed
with shame, he succumbs shortly thereafter to a stroke.

To appreciate the ambiguity of Myshkin one must see the
close relation of this character to Stavrogin in *Demons*. The
two men are antitheses of each other. Both are uprooted
aristocrats; both remain outside the frantic agitation that
they arouse. Both are masters of the game that they are not
concerned to win. But Stavrogin is different from Myshkin
in being cruel and insensitive. The suffering of others leaves
him indifferent, unless, perhaps, he takes a perverse pleasure in it. He is young, handsome, rich, and intelligent; he
has received more than his share of all the gifts that nature
and society can confer on an individual. That is why he lives
in the most complete boredom: he has no more desires, for
he has possessed everything.

Here it is necessary to give up the traditional view that
insists on the "autonomy" of the characters in fiction. The
notebooks of Dostoevsky demonstrate that Myshkin and
Stavrogin have a common origin. These two characters embody contradictory responses, because they are hypothetical
responses to one and only one question: the spiritual mean-

ing of detachment. Behind this abstract literary expression
it is necessary to have recourse to the examination of moral
consciousness that *Notes from the Underground* inaugu-
rated and that will attain even profounder levels until and
including *The Brothers Karamazov.*

What is Dostoevsky's life situation during the period of
The Idiot and *Demons?* The revelation of the underground
is the revelation of nihilism. At this time Dostoevsky's religion was hardly anything other than an extreme reaction to
the influence of Belinsky, a refusal of the intellectual atheism that raged among Russian intellectuals. It is necessary
to recognize that the writer is given over to nihilism, but
this nihilism is more than a burden; it is a source of knowledge and even power in a world which still believes in the
solidity of romantic values.

We can easily verify the effectiveness of the revelation
of the underground in the literary domain. This period is
the most fruitful that Dostoevsky had ever known, and the
works published during this time are infinitely superior to
the preceding ones. The new life the writer discovered for
himself after prison was never contradicted. But Dostoevsky's existence, always unstable and disorderly, passes then
through a paroxysm of instability and disorder. The energy
of this nihilism seems to be particularly directed, quite para-
doxically, against the most varied forms of self-destruction.

But there is something else: if Dostoevsky typically played
the role of the one conquered, as early in the 1860s with
Pauline Suslova for example, he nonetheless also succeeded
in having his own way as he never before could have done.
His personality as a man and a writer asserted itself each
day with more authority, and he already exercised influence
over the most diverse milieus. He no longer represents a

short-lived fad, an illusion quickly dissipated, as in 1846. Many aspects of his existence escape the grasp of the Other, the type of enslavement to the Other that defines the underground. The creation of a Myshkin and a Stavrogin reflects this change. Dostoevsky becomes interested henceforth as much, if not perhaps more, in characters who dominate as in those who are dominated. It is astonishing that the novelist could have united in himself the two contrary characters, Myshkin and Stavrogin. Was his personality utterly monstrous? But we must understand that the difference between Myshkin and Stavrogin is simultaneously immense and minuscule. It finally comes down to a question of perspective.

Faced with Myshkin's remarkable success with women, his rival for Aglaya wonders whether the prince is not the most cunning and diabolical of men rather than the simplest. A somewhat similar incident happens in *Demons*. The limping woman, a person half mad but inspired, whom Stavrogin has married out of bravado, at first sees in him the hero and saint who must emerge one day to save Russia. It is therefore possible to ask oneself whether Myshkin is not Stavrogin and, reciprocally, whether Stavrogin is not Myshkin. The most extreme pride, even if it does not encounter an obstacle and avoids falling into the masochistic trap, is always the most difficult to perceive because it really scorns the vulgar satisfactions that vanity claims. It is more easily confused with authentic humility than are all the intermediary attitudes. Consequently, nothing is easier than to misjudge these two extremes, both in oneself and in others. This is not to say that Dostoevsky should be taken successively, or alternately, for Myshkin and Stavrogin, but these two characters constitute the fictional flowering of the two points of view between which the writer hesitates as he reflects on the moral significance of his own behavior.

The project of writing *The Idiot*, conceiving a hero whom his perfection, not his imperfection, separates from others — this is to affirm his own innocence and to transfer all his guilt onto others. Inversely, the project of writing *Demons*, conceiving a hero whose detachment is a form of moral and spiritual degradation — this is to refuse the former kind of justification, to refuse to read any superiority whatever into the lucidity that dismantles and reassembles the dimensions of the underground. The "detachment" does not prove that one has conquered one's own pride; it proves only that one has exchanged slavery for mastery. The roles are reversed but the structure of intersubjective relations remains the same.

This double creation reveals, indeed, the type of person Dostoevsky was. He cannot be satisfied with the relative autonomy that manages to win a victory over the swarming chaos of the underground. It is not enough for him to see the eternal misunderstanding between the Self and the Other play itself out to his advantage rather to his disadvantage as an author. It is the misunderstanding itself that he sees as intolerable. Nihilism is unable to destroy in him the need to unify and communicate.

Myshkin and Stavrogin are essentially two contrasting images of the novelist. *The Idiot* and *Demons* are circular novels; they are developed from the starting point of a central threshold around which the novelistic world gravitates. This is an image of aesthetic creation, but the meaning of this creation changes from one novel to the other. If in writing *The Idiot* Dostoevsky had not gone beyond his initial idea of the perfect man, we would readily say that *Demons* is to *The Idiot* what *Notes from the Underground* is to *The Insulted and Injured*. We find there a new rupture that is brought about at a more elevated level than the prior one and whose aesthetic and spiritual fruits will be accordingly even more remarkable.

This summary analysis scarcely touches the surface of the "existential" meaning of the works considered; it would be necessary to take into account, in particular, all the secondary characters. We have sought only to show that Dostoevsky's creative work is always bound to a feverish interrogation that bears on the creator himself and on his relations with others. The characters are always the X's and Y's of equations that are concerned to define these relations.

࿔

There are likewise *models* for Stavrogin. It is possible to recognize the elements borrowed from them without denying the profoundly subjective character of the novelist's creative work. Knowledge of oneself is perpetually mediated by knowledge of others. The distinction between the "autobiographical" characters and those that are not is thus superficial; it grasps only the superficial works, those that succeed neither in revealing the preexisting mediations between the Other and the Self nor in making themselves the vehicle of new mediations. If the work is profound, one can no more speak of "autobiography" than of "invention" or "imagination" in the usual sense of these terms.

One important model for Stavrogin is Nikolay Speshnev, one of the members of the Petrashevsky circle. Associating with this revolutionary group in the late 1840s cost the novelist his four years in prison. Son of a rich landowner,

Speshnev had spent much time traveling in Europe. The
testimonies of the period are agreed in recognizing in him
"Byronian" manners, "splendid and sinister" at the same
time, very much like the character of *Demons*. Petrashevsky
called Speshnev "the man of masks," and Bakunin admired
his lordly style. If we are to believe the story told much later
by the author's friend and doctor Yanosky, in the period of
the Petrashevsky circle Dostoevsky would have recognized a
mysterious bond linking him to Speshnev: "I am with him
and I belong to him," the writer would have affirmed; "I
have my Mephistopheles."

Speshnev played a role with Dostoevsky somewhat like
that of Shidlovsky some years earlier. It is this role of
master to disciple that one finds in this novel between Stavrogin and all those who are possessed. The underground
mimetism, the imitation of the rival frequently noted in the
preceding works, acquires in this novel an intellectual, spiritual, and even "religious" dimension. Dostoevsky unveils
the irrational element that occurs in the diffusion of every
message, even if this message intends to be entirely rational.
A new point of view does not gain an audience with the
masses unless it awakens the enthusiasm of true believers.

All those possessed hang on every word of this negative messiah that Stavrogin is. All speak of him in religious
terms. Stavrogin is their "light," their "star"; they bow before him as "before the Most High." The petitions directed
to him are very humble prayers. "You know," says Shatov to his idol, "I kiss your footprint when you go out. I
cannot tear you from my heart, Nikolay Stavrogin." Peter
Verkhovensky himself, whose entire philosophy consists of
not being duped by anything, engages in an act of religious
submission to this enigmatic person:

You, you are my idol. You offend no one and yet everyone hates you; you treat people as equals but they are
afraid of you.... You are the head, you are the sun, and
me, I am nothing but an earthworm.

Stavrogin is to all his satellites what the insolent officer
is to the underground man, the unsurpassable obstacle of
whom one finally makes an absolute when one wants to
be absolute oneself. The theme of the obstacle, like all the
underground themes, acquires in *Demons* a quasi-mythical
dimension. Stavrogin agrees to hold a duel, or rather, to
serve as a target for a man whose father he gravely insulted.
He shows such indifference to the bullets of his adversary
that the latter, greatly shaken, is not even capable of aim-
ing. This is precisely the mastery of oneself that permits
domination of the underground.

The desire for union with the abhorred rival discloses
here its fundamental meaning. The one filled with pride does
not renounce being god; indeed, this is why he bows down
before Stavrogin in a spirit of hatred. He constantly returns
to bruise himself against the obstacle, for he believes only in
him; he wants to become him. The extraordinary baseness
of the underground character, his paralysis in the presence
of his rival, his consternation at the idea of the conflict that
he himself provoked — all this, in the light of *Demons*, certainly does not become rational, but perfectly intelligible
and coherent. The "dream of the life à trois" is particularly
significant. The disciple renounces conquering the women
whom the idol covets. He thus makes himself his servant —
it is tempting to say, his pimp — in the hope that he will be
able to gather up the crumbs from the heavenly banquet.

Since it is the idol's characteristic to thwart and persecute its worshipers, any contact with it is not possible without suffering. Masochism and sadism constitute the sacraments of the underground mystique. Submitting to suffering reveals to the masochist the nearness of the divine executioner, and inflicting suffering gives the sadist the illusion of embodying this executioner in the exercise of his sacred power.

The worship that the ones possessed render to Stavrogin is one of those themes that sometimes lead to judging Dostoevsky too *Russian* for Western minds. However, Dostoevsky adds nothing to the purely psychological descriptions of the underground. *Demons* articulates explicitly a meaning already implicit in all the preceding works. Is it not correct, for example, to see Trusotsky's journey to St. Petersburg as a kind of vile pilgrimage? One might say that this is simply a metaphor. Perhaps, but from metaphor to metaphor, this is a vision singularly coherent which finally asserts itself. The "unnatural" attempts of the eternal husband to lead the woman of his choice to the feet of the idol resemble the sacrifices of primitive religions closely enough to be mistaken for them. They resemble the barbaric rites that the cults of blood, sex, and the night demand of their devotees. The possessed, too, lead their women to Stavrogin's bed.

The religious character of underground passion is found in *The Gambler,* but it is a woman who describes the *utchitel,* and in fact the language of this book should not surprise us, for it is through and through the language of the Western poetic tradition. But it should not be forgotten that the troubadours borrowed this language from Christian mysticism. The great poets of the Western world, from the Middle Ages to Baudelaire and Claudel, have never confused this mystical imagery with simple rhetoric. They have, rather, been able to preserve or recover some of the original power of the sacred, whether to savor it or to denounce therein its blasphemous connotations. Behind the passionate rhetoric that he has utilized since his early works, Dostoevsky now discovers quite an idolatrous depth; in the same act of discovery he enters deeply into the metaphysical truth of his own destiny and climbs toward the profound sources of the Western poetic mystery.

Underground life is a hate-filled imitation of Stavrogin. The latter, whose name means "bearer of the cross," usurps the place of Christ with the ones possessed. With Peter Verkhovensky he forms the Spirit of subversion, and with Stepan Verkhovensky, father of Peter and spiritual father of Stavrogin (he was his tutor), he forms a sort of demoniac counter-trinity. The universe of hate parodies, in the least details, the universe of divine love. Stavrogin and the possessed whom he brings along in his train are all in quest of a wrong-way redemption whose theological name is damnation. Dostoevsky recovers, in inverse fashion, the great symbols of Scripture, such as those developed in patristic and medieval exegesis. Spiritual structures themselves are *doubles*. All the images, metaphors, and symbols that describe them have a double meaning, and one must interpret them in opposing fashion according as the structures are oriented toward what is high, toward unity, toward God, as in Christian life, or toward what is low, as in *Demons*, i.e., toward the duality that leads to fragmentation and finally to the total destruction of personal being.

Stavrogin is to the possessed what the woman is to the lover, what the rival is to the one consumed with jealousy, what roulette is to the gambler; and so likewise to Raskolnikov is the image of Napoleon, in whom Hegel already saw "the living incarnation of divinity." Stavrogin is the synthesis of all the prior underground relationships. The novelist does not add anything nor subtract anything. The rigor he demonstrates is that of the phenomenologist who brings the essence or the reason out of a whole series of phenomena. It is not accurate to say that he interprets; it is rather the manner of gathering and comparing these phenomena that discloses their profound common identity, catching suddenly a thousand scattered assumptions in one brilliant configuration of evidence.

Whoever revolts against God in order to adore himself always ends up adoring the Other, Stavrogin. This intuition, elementary but profound, succeeds in metaphysically surpassing the underground psychology begun in *Crime and Punishment*. Raskolnikov is basically the person who does not attain the goal of taking the place of the god he has killed, but the meaning of his failure remains hidden. It is this meaning that *Demons* reveals. Stavrogin is neither god *in himself* nor even *for himself*. The unanimous tributes of the possessed are the tributes of slaves, and as such they are devoid of all value. Stavrogin is god *for the Others*.

Dostoevsky is not a philosopher, but a novelist. He does not create the character of Stavrogin because he formulated for himself, intellectually, the unity of all the underground phenomena; to the contrary, he succeeds in relating this unity because he created the character of Stavrogin. Underground psychology tends in its own right toward structures which are increasingly more stable and rigid. Mastery attracts mastery and slavery attracts slavery. Not seeming to desire anything, the master meets only slaves about him and, in meeting only slaves, he cannot desire anything. This is the implacable logic of underground psychology which leads to metaphysics.

But Dostoevsky's intuition has also a philosophical import, an intuition calling for a dialogue with every form of Western individualism, from Descartes to Nietzsche. It calls for this dialogue even more insistently to the extent that one recovers in these two great prophets of individualism an experience of the Double similar to that of Dostoevsky.

We turn to the biography of Baillet, as does Georges Poulet in his *Etudes sur le temps humain,** in order to set in relief all the self-divisions that the Cartesian experience involves. This critic shows us that "in the intoxication of Descartes, there is...a shadow side and there is a light side....These two sides are...tragically dissociated." The mind of the philosopher is affected by a "pendulum movement"; it suffers "the alternate swings of cyclothymia." Poulet speaks even of the "enemy brother" whom the philosopher harbors in his breast. He describes "the great misfortune of a time torn between a mind which is situated in nontemporal reality and the remainder who live only an obscure and indistinct duration." Beside the "dominating" Descartes here is a Descartes "swept off his route by a power that dominates him and transcends him." This is to say that "we enter into that dark country of anxiety...which subsists subterraneously in us and whose action upon us never ceases." It should be understood that this experience of underground division is strictly bound to what is most fundamental in the philosopher's conduct. "One in its goal, his research was double in its method."

---

*"Le songe de Descartes," in *Etudes sur le temps humain* (Paris: Plon, 1950), 16–47.

Baillet describes Descartes's bizarre manner of walking as it appears to him in the *Songe* (Dream): "Believing he was walking along the streets, he had to lean to the left side so that he could proceed to the place where he wanted to go, because he felt a great weakness on his right side on which he was unable to support himself."

Georges Poulet sees in this conduct the "symbolic image of a life divided in two." How can one avoid thinking here of Ivan Karamazov, the most "divided" perhaps of all Dostoevsky's characters, who himself also walks in an unbalanced gait? Alyosha watches his brother walk away and observes that his right shoulder is lower than his left shoulder.

There is, finally, a passage in Baillet's essay that seems to describe the very hallucination of *The Double*: "Having perceived that he had passed a man of his acquaintance without greeting him, he wanted to turn back on his steps to make a sign of civility to him, but he was driven back violently by the wind that blew against the church."

This silent encounter resembles likewise the famous Rapallo vision (January 1883) that "gave" to Nietzsche the persona of Zarathustra. On the route to Portofino the writer saw his hero appear and pass him without saying a word to him. Nietzsche evoked this strange event in a poem which lets no doubt exist concerning the nature of the experience:

> Then, suddenly friend! one became two! —
> And Zarathustra passed by beside me.

In the course of its history Western individualism took over little by little the prerogatives that had belonged to God in medieval philosophy. This is not a matter of a simple philosophical mode, a passing infatuation for the subjective.

Since Descartes, there is no longer any point of departure except the *cogito ergo sum*. Kant succeeded for a time in keeping the watergates of subjectivism closed; he managed this with a completely arbitrary compromise, but the truth must out and it does so with a bang. Absolute idealism and Promethean thought will push Cartesianism to its extreme consequences.

What is this omnipotence that is inherited, with the arrival of the modern world, not by human beings in general nor by the sum of all individuals, but by each one of us in particular? What is this God who is in the process of dying? It is the Jehovah of the Bible, the jealous God of the Hebrews, the one who tolerates no rivals. The question is far from being merely historical and academic. It has to do actually with determining the meaning of the enterprise that demands total payment of each of us, modern individuals. Every form of pluralism is here excluded. It is the one and unique God of the Jewish-Christian tradition who gives his particular stamp to Western individualism. Each mode of subjectivity must found and justify the being of the real in his totality and affirm *I am who I am*. Modern philosophy recognizes this demand when it makes of subjectivity the only source of being, but this recognition remains abstract. Nietzsche and Dostoevsky are the only ones to understand that the task is properly superhuman, even if it imposes itself upon all of us. The self-divinization, the crucifixion that it implies, constitutes immediate reality, the daily bread of all the little St. Petersburg bureaucrats who pass with no transition from the medieval universe to contemporary nihilism.

Here the question really is *who* will be the heir, the only son of the dead God. The idealist philosophers believe that it is enough to respond in terms of the self or subject to resolve the problem. But the Self is not an *object* alongside other selves, for it is constituted by its relation to the Other and cannot be considered outside of this relation. It is this relation which the effort to substitute oneself for the God of Bible always corrupts. Divinity cannot become identified either with the Self or with the Other; it is perpetually part of the struggle *between* the Self and the Other. Sexuality, ambition, literature — all intersubjective relations — become burdened with this underground battle.

We can no longer fail to recognize the effects of this metaphysical poisoning, for they unceasingly grow worse. These effects have made themselves felt, in a concealed but recognizable fashion, well before the twentieth and even the nineteenth centuries. Perhaps it is most suitable to seek the first traces of our malaise in the very origin of the era of the individualist, in that morality of *generosity* that Descartes, the first philosopher of individualism, and Corneille, its first dramatist, developed at the same time. As Lucien Goldmann has quite rightly remarked in his *Mediations,* Descartes cannot strictly justify his principle of generosity, because he cannot deduce it from the *cogito.*

It is significant that rationalist individualism and the irrational morality of generosity appear conjointly. If one considers this "generosity" in light of *Demons,* one will see there perhaps the beginning of an "underground" dynamic whose moments correspond to the metamorphoses of morality and sensibility, as they work themselves out into the contemporary period.

The Self whose vocation is to divinize itself refuses to recognize the fearsome problem that the presence of others poses; it is even less likely to seek to resolve this problem at the practical level, outside of philosophical reflection. In the early stages of the dynamic, the Self feels itself strong enough to triumph over its rivals. But still it must prove to itself its superiority. In order that the proof sought may be satisfying in its own eyes, the rivalry must be honest. The solution asserted is evidently generosity. It is necessary to respect the rules of "fair play" and to gain agreement from the Other that it respects them equally so that victor and vanquished be cleanly judged and distinguished. "The general interest" is always alleged to be the goal, as it is necessary to dissimulate the egotistic object of this maneuver.

The morality of generosity is much less "underground" than the moralities that succeed it, but it is already underground in the sense that the Self imposes on itself the regime of *proof*. It actually believes in its own divinity, i.e., in its superiority over others, but it does not believe in it sufficiently to dispense with a concrete demonstration. It needs to reassure itself.

The transition from the Cartesian "generosity" to the pre-romantic "sensibility" is connected with a serious worsening of the conflict between the selves. The Self is incapable of reducing the Other, all the others, to slavery. The "divinity" that remained more or less solidly anchored in the Self during the first century of individualism tends henceforth to become displaced toward the Other. In order to avoid this catastrophe, which is otherwise imminent, the Self tries an arrangement with its rivals. It does not renounce individualism, but it seeks to neutralize its consequences. It endeavors to sign a non-aggression pact with the Other. At the end of the eighteenth century everyone threw themselves into the arms of the others, as if to delay the great fury of the Revolution and the triumph of unbridled rivalry; but this cushioning of the effects is purely tactical and has nothing to do with true love.

Corneillan "generosity" took on a nuance of hysteria. One should not be astonished that sadism and masochism then triumph in literature. Contemporaries are rarely aware of what is happening because they themselves take part in the same kind of game. Diderot, for example, is ecstatic over the "nobility" and the "delicacy" of Richardson's literary characters. The rupture between interpretation and the objective meaning of the work recalls what we have observed with regard to *The Insulted and Injured*.

It is at the end of the eighteenth century that Christianity, simply repudiated by the French philosophers, reappeared in inverted form in the underground. This is when the romantic "Manicheanism" raged for the first time, and only the greatest novelists are immune from it. Literature becomes "subjective" and "objective" and the underground self-divisions multiply. A little later the Double itself, whose presence corresponds to a paroxysm of tearing apart between the Self and the Other, makes its appearance among the most agonizing and anguished of the writers. Literature is mobilized in the conflict of the Self and the Other, beginning to play its justificatory role which we still note in it in our time. Rousseau affirms that he will present himself armed with *The Confessions* before the supreme tribunal. The Book of Life is displaced by the book of his life.

Shortly before his final rupture with Dostoevsky, Belinsky wrote to one of his friends, "I have just read *The Confessions* of Rousseau, and all through them I experienced the greatest repugnance for this gentleman, so much does he resemble Dostoevsky, who believes that all the human race envies and persecutes him."

The author draws unfair consequences from the comparison, but states therein a profound truth. The lucidity of Dostoevsky the genius is not given but won through conquest; and we will comprehend that this conquest was not at all predetermined, that it is almost miraculous, in fact, once we recognize that the work of Rousseau reflects, without ever completely revealing, obsessions quite similar to those of the Russian writer. The major work of the "dream of the life à trois" is *The New Heloise*. This novel sets in play the same elements as *The Insulted and Injured,* and one can read it also in the light of *The Eternal Husband.* For Rousseau as for Dostoevsky, obsession with sexual inferiority pushes the Self into rivalry, but forbids it at the same time to become deeply engaged with it; the highly emotional fraternity with the Other dissimulates this conflict somewhat, but it does not suppress it. Maria, the new Heloise of Kuznetsk, is less elegant, less harmonious, more grating than the one of Clarens, but she is not less strongly felt.

Although it goes back to Rousseau, the rhetoric of *The Insulted and Injured* is not superimposed on experience which could be first apprehended in its pristine state. Rhetoric and experience are finally one. It is precisely this that the Siberian correspondence reveals. The romanticism of the early Dostoevsky should not be conceived as a simple literary error easily corrected the day the writer finally discovers "his way." Besides, there was not a way, for nobody had yet opened one. Rousseau never wrote the equivalent of *The Eternal Husband.* French romanticism possessed its *Confessions of a Child of the Century* (Alfred de Musset), but it still awaited its *Notes from the Underground.* Dostoevsky's work of genius is the fragment of truth that emerges suddenly against the immense backdrop of self-deception.

The early Dostoevsky lied to himself, of course, but the self-deception he reenacts is what all the fashionable productions murmured to him, all the worldly conversations — even, one is tempted to say, what nature itself seemed to whisper. This Dostoevsky tries to live his relations with himself and with others at the same level of consciousness as the cultivated people around him. But it is because he did not succeed in this attempt that he is a bad romantic and that he bears within himself the opportunity of an exceptional destiny. He is not a bad romantic because he lacks the essence of romanticism but, to the contrary, because he possesses it in superabundance, because he is always ready to rush into madness or genius. He conceives himself as the grimacing *double* of the proper and distinguished writers à la Turgenev, i.e., of all the good pupils of Western romanticism. The contradictions that define romanticism are too violent in him for him to hold them in respect. In *Notes* the underground character describes the mechanism of this failure, and he assimilates his case to Russian romanticism in general. Russians, he writes, are incapable of holding to "the beautiful and the sublime" to the end; they always show, at least a little, that sordid part of themselves that would be appropriate to conceal. They finally come across as real Russian peasants by committing some error of taste, some enormous buffoonery which destroys the dignity and solemnity of their own theater.

The Russian imitation of European models is always a little strained, constantly ready to turn into parody. Russians therefore have no choice but between the grossest literary artifices and inspired realism. When it comes to their own literary and spiritual tendencies, the great Russian romantics demonstrate a clairvoyance quite rare among their European analogues. Pushkin writes *Eugeny Oniegin,* Gogol *The Dead Souls,* Lermontov *A Hero of Our Time.* And Dostoevsky finally, the most unbalanced of all, is doubtlessly the most inspired. With him mimetic rivalry takes a form so acute that none of the masks that it borrows succeeds in obscuring it lastingly. Accordingly, the writer never disposes of the minimum of equilibrium and stability necessary to the creation of a work of "talent."

The Russia of 1840 was to some extent "behind" Europe. It confused, in a very significant way, romantic baroque, Rousseau-like sensibility, *Sturm und Drang,* and the romanticism of 1830. The young Dostoevsky devours, pell-mell, *The Brigands* by Schiller, *Notre Dame de Paris, Chatterton,* Lamartine, Byron, and...Corneille. This last choice surprises us because Westerners are used to distinguishing carefully the diverse periods of their literary history. From the child who would have declared at the age of six, "I want to be god," it is an easy transition to the adolescent who declaims, "I am the master of myself as of the universe," a line taken from Corneille. This same adolescent would write then to his brother Michael, "And Corneille? Have you read *The Cid?* Read it, you wretch, read it and fall to your knees before Corneille. You have offended him."

It is remarkable that Dostoevsky, from his adolescence to his old age, would have traveled through all the moments of a mythology of the Self that are displayed over almost three centuries in western Europe. This prodigious consummation of individualist myths confirms, furthermore, the unity of modern sensibility. If, beginning with *Notes from the Underground,* Dostoevsky surmounts the properly romantic modalities of individualism by describing them, some new modalities, particularly Promethean superhumanity, be-

gin to obsess him. In 1863 the Russian writer was still
thirty, fifty, or even two hundred years behind his German
or French contemporaries. Yet in some few years he will
have caught and passed everyone, having rejected the myth
of the superhuman before it had even seized Occidental
imaginings!

જ

One reads occasionally that religious prejudice has warped
the meaning of *Demons* and that the novelist would not
have escaped from nihilism if he had remained faithful to
his better intuitions. This is a double error. The first consists
in separating Christian symbolism from the novelistic structure. We have seen that the truths painfully extracted from
the psychological underground call for this symbolism; they
are organized upon contact with it and they discover therein
a form that suits them — their natural aesthetic form, one
could say. This agreement between the symbolism and the
psychology is all the more remarkable given that the psychology, in the realm of Dostoevky's creativity, is anterior to
the symbolism. The novelist does not attempt to "illustrate"
the principles of Christian faith, but he obeys the internal
dynamics of his own creation.

The second error consists in believing that having recourse to Christian symbolism is incompatible with nihilism. The conjunction of the symbolism and the psychology
demonstrates that modern consciousness remains caught in
a Christian "form," even when it flatters itself that it has
escaped Christianity, but it demonstrates nothing else. The
Dostoevsky of *Demons* has more or less exorcised rationalism, scientism, and utilitarianism, which dominated then in
all of Europe, but he is not certain that he has exorcised

nihilism. Certain critics of Dostoevsky have the tendency to hurry the rhythm of his spiritual evolution, whether because they desire superficially to "Christianize" his work or, to the contrary, because they desire to de-Christianize it for their own convenience. For Dostoevsky writing is a means of knowing, an instrument of exploration; it is thus always beyond the author himself, ahead of his intelligence and his faith. To say this is to say again that Dostoevsky is essentially a novelist.

Christian choice may be deduced from the madness and failure of the possessed. But what is this deduction worth in light of the immense liturgy of evil that is deployed from one end to the other of this masterwork? The platitudes of utilitarianism and modern pragmatism are definitively swept away, but the story seems to be delivered over to satanic powers.

It is the triumph of Satan that the possessed proclaim. The belief in the power of the devil should have as its counterpart a still firmer faith in the power of grace. Dostoevsky is distressed not to experience this firmness in himself. The writer sees himself fascinated by evil and he wonders if anything good could come to him from this source. To discover something of Satan's presence everywhere, is this not to play his game, to collaborate in his work of division — even more effectively, perhaps, than if one marched under his flag? *Is it possible to believe in the devil without believing in God?* This question that Stavrogin poses to Tikhon leads us to the very heart of the work, for it is the question that Dostoevsky asks himself.

Lebedyev, in *The Idiot,* is a cowardly character, but he is also an interpreter of the book of Revelation intoxicated with prophetic pessimism. He applies the sacred text strikingly to contemporary events. He has some disciples, including a peaceful retired general who has just died. Speculating that his lessons had something to do with his death, the instructor experiences a great satisfaction.

Lebedyev is only a buffoon, but his buffooneries are connected to the examination of conscience that the novelist pursues through various characters in all his great works. *The Idiot* discloses a kind of preoccupation that opens up fully in *Demons*, i.e., in the novel of Dostoevsky that is the most marked by the apocalyptic spirit and prophetic pessimism. The artist wonders whether he does not mix something impure into his personal indignation and whether the ardent, eternal need that we all have to justify ourselves does not manifest itself here in a new form. This anxiety allows us to see one more proof of the profoundly logical character of Dostoevsky's creative work.

To bring to light the dialogue of the novelist with himself, it is necessary to renounce bending the work either in the direction of skepticism or in the direction of a faith monolithic and a priori which would be, perhaps, the contrary of authentic faith. We must follow, in its movement toward Christ, the progress of this terribly demanding religious conscience, for it cannot be satisfied with half-measures or pretenses.

It is Shatov in *Demons* who most resembles his creator by his political and religious attitude, by his character, and even by his physical appearance. Shatov is awkward and ugly, but upright. We recognize in the Slavophil and orthodox theories of the repentant revolutionary the ideology that the novelist defended in his *Diary of a Writer*. Shatov's wife lived with Stavrogin but has returned to her husband and given birth to a child. We encounter Shatov in the pe-

riod just before he is assassinated by his former political
allies. His happiness conveys to us an echo of the content-
ment and peace that Dostoevsky finally knew in his family
life, after his second marriage.

To Stavrogin, who asks him whether he believes in God,
Shatov does not respond directly. He believes "in orthodox
Russia," in "the Russian Christ"; he believes that "his Second Coming will take place in Russia." He never affirms
that he believes in God; the most he dares to say is that
he *will* believe. Before holding, as is often done, that the
"avowals" of Shatov contradict the "message" of the novel,
it is fitting to specify the nature of this message.

Shatov's idea, like all the ideas of *Demons*, was planted
by Stavrogin. That is, it remains a tributary of the nihilism
that it claims to combat. It is not tradition but ideology of
tradition. Nihilism is the source of all ideologies because it
is the source of all the underground divisions and oppositions. This is why the ideas that Stavrogin disseminates
round about him all contradict themselves. Shatov is against
Occidentalism, against the Revolution, against his former
friends. The Slavophil credo intends to be entirely positive
but, despite appearances, the *against* precedes the *for* within
it and determines it.

The "avowals" of Shatov do not reveal a "disbelief"
which would be immutable, underlying belief in the way
the Freudian unconscious underlies consciousness; they embody, rather, a moment of the spiritual dialectic of Dostoevsky. By its origins and function the Slavophil "idea" is
as far removed from Christ as in France the ideology of
the Restoration would be. One must realize this in order
to advance in the way of true Christianity.

If the rationalist, "the man of the Crystal Palace," were

able to understand that the Judeo-Christian pattern is rooted in him much more profoundly than his own negations, he would certainly bow down before the divine mystery. But the nihilist is of another temper. The vision of *Demons* is no longer compatible, assuredly, with certain coarse refutations of Christianity, but it confirms the tragic failure of this religion. It may therefore lead to an indictment more harsh than all the criticisms of the past.

The engineer Kirillov raises this indictment. According to him, all evil comes from the desire for immortality that Christ has foolishly sparked in us. It is this desire, never satisfied, that puts human existence in disequilibrium and produces the underground. It is this desire that Kirillov wants to destroy with one sole blow by his philosophical suicide. He kills himself not in despair of not being immortal, like so many others, but in order to possess the infinity of his freedom in the total acceptance of finitude. Like Raskolnikov, Kirillov is a Nietzschean hero who hopes to transcend the underground thanks to a pride the like of which one could not conceive as greater or purer. It is the same conflict as in *Crime and Punishment,* but here nihilism and Christianity have both grown greater. One could say that they confer strength on one another. Kirillov searches no longer for the absolute in killing his fellow human, as Raskolnikov did, but in killing himself.

To understand the "idea" of Kirillov, one should recognize there a superior form of that "anti-redemption" which all the disciples of Stavrogin pursue more or less consciously. The death of this possessed person must put an end to the Christian era, but at the same time it intends to be very much like, yet radically different from the passion of Christ. Kirillov is so convinced of the metaphysical efficacy of his gesture that he is indifferent to all publicity: *Quidquid latet apparebit* (Whatever is hidden will appear)....He does not imitate Christ, he parodies him. He does not seek to collaborate in the work of redemption but to correct it. Underground ambivalence is here borne to the highest degree of intensity and spiritual meaning, for the rival who is simultaneously venerated and hated is the Redeemer himself. To the humble imitation of Jesus Christ is opposed the prideful and satanic imitation of the possessed. The very essence of the underground is finally revealed.

Chapter 4

Resurrection

The Shatov episode commences an overcoming of Slavophil ideology, and with the Kirillov episode is begun an overcoming of nihilism, both of which will be accomplished in *The Brothers Karamazov* (1880). The serenity of the last novel is far removed from *Demons*. The spirit of Stavrogin breathes through the vengeful caricatures which are sprinkled throughout the latter narrative, for example, that of the elder Verkhovensky or that of the writer Karmazinov, in whom it is not difficult to recognize Turgenev, the longtime literary enemy. The rancors accumulated since Dostoevsky's literary debut come up to the surface. Some of the utterances of *Demons* come from Belinsky himself, and we find them also in the correspondence. This critic avowed himself ready, for example, "in order to make even perhaps only a fraction of humanity happy, to destroy the rest by iron and by fire." He professed a radical atheism: "I don't see in the words 'God' and 'religion' anything but obscurantism, shadows, chains, and instruments of torture," he wrote to Herzen in 1845. Feodor Mikhailovich, though horrified by his attacks against Christ, was profoundly marked by his social messianism.

The novel borrows its intrigue from contemporary events and owes the main bulk of its material to recollections from the Petrashevsky circle, but it is completely directed against

the man who dominated the existence of Dostoevsky for
many long years. One can hardly doubt that the young
writer projected on Belinsky, the redeemer, the man responsible for his passage from nothingness to being, filial feelings
that were never realized during the life of his father. After
his rupture with the Turgenev group Dostoevsky continued
for some time to frequent Belinsky, but the critic finally,
with all the others, took a dislike to his former protégé.
He condemned all the writings after *Poor Folk,* and he even
came to the point of repudiating the praise he so impru-
dently poured out on this first work. Here, for instance, is
what he wrote to one of his friends about the Dostoevsky
of *The Landlady:* "He is the worst of the inept! ... Each of
his new works is a new catastrophe. ... We were rudely deceived about the genius of Dostoevsky. ... I myself, the first
of the critics, was nothing but a silly ass."

With its mixture of truth and falsehood, of lucidity and
naive pride, the letter itself is from the underground. After having conferred the fulness of existence on the young
writer, Belinsky repudiates this unworthy son and plunges
him once more into nothingness. From then on Dostoevsky
experienced for the critic a mixture of veneration and hate
of the typically underground sort. If he begins to associate
with *true* revolutionaries, it is not from reasoned conviction
but to enter into a fervently militant rivalry with the inacces-
sible model. In the Petrashevsky circle where they conspired
in a committed though abstract fashion, he became notable
for the extremism of his opinions. He passed as a person
"capable of leading a riot brandishing a red flag." One day
he declared himself in favor of a rebel army of the Russian
peasantry. But his literary work does not convey to us, as it
were, any echo of this political furor. Censorship does not

suffice to explicate this silence. In 1848 Dostoevsky published *A Weak Heart* and *White Nights,* and the anguish
that comes to expression in these works has nothing to do
with the revolutionary movements that shook Europe and
provoked the enthusiasm of the Russian intelligentsia. It is,
then, a *double* existence that Dostoevsky is leading; all of
the ideological side of his being is an imitation of Belinsky.
His public life stems from a veritable bewitchment.

On April 15, 1849, Dostoevsky read to the Petrashevsky
circle a seditious letter of Belinsky to Gogol. The future informer on the circle was present and he was later to accuse
Dostoevsky of having put into this reading an extraordinary
passion and conviction. Dostoevsky, in turn, defends himself very sincerely against the perception that he approves
the text of the letter, but the arguments he invokes are not
convincing:

> The one who has denounced me, is he able to say
> to which of the two correspondents I was more at-
> tached [Belinsky or Gogol]?...I beseech you now to
> consider the following: would I have read an article
> of a man with whom I had become embroiled over
> a question of ideas (this is not a secret, many people
> know of it) by presenting it as a breviary, as a formu-
> lary for everyone to follow?...In reading I tried not
> to give any preference for the one or the other of the
> correspondents.

The informer had all the trumps in his hand. Why would
he have introduced into his report a lie which could only
have weakened it? He speaks the truth and we are astonished, with Henri Troyat, to see Dostoevsky lend "his voice
and his talent to the prose of an *enemy.*" It is futile, how-

ever, to seek the explication of this enigma at the level of ideology. Belinsky is the metaphysical rival, the monstrous idol whom Dostoevsky tries in vain to incarnate. Hate is thus not incompatible with passionate imitation; it is even its inevitable counterpart. The two feelings are contradictory only in appearance, or rather it is in underground pride, as always, that one must search for the key to the contradiction. One will not explicate Dostoevsky's work with his biography, but one will finally perhaps, thanks to the creative work, render the biography really intelligible.

After his release from prison Dostoevsky turns away, first hesitantly, then fiercely, from the spiritual heritage transmitted by Belinsky. He then discovers that the revolutionary ideas that he flaunted and that brought him to condemnation were never truly *his*. The ideology of *Demons* is entirely copied and imitated: "The most important force, the cement that connects everything together, is the shame of holding one's own opinion." Abandoning the ideology of a Belinsky, like abandoning, in the same period, sentimental and romantic rhetoric, is the fruit of that implacable examination of conscience to which we owe all the great works. If Dostoevsky does not convey to us the entire truth, he brings us certainly *his* truth when he links revolutionary behavior to the prestige mediated by an irresistible seducer rather than to an authentic passion for freedom.

The feelings Belinsky inspired in his young admirer were wrenching to the prior foundations of his life. In letting himself be "adopted" by the cosmopolitan thinker, revolutionary, and atheist, Dostoevsky necessarily had the sense that he was betraying the memory of his father, who would have been appalled by Belinsky's ideas. The critic's influence reenforced the son's feeling of guilt toward his father.

Each time he incited revolt, even if only in thought, against the national and religious tradition, i.e., against the paternal tradition, the master appeared to his disciple as the instigator of a new *parricide*. The association between Belinsky and parricide is strengthened still more in Czarist Russia by the blasphemous character of any attack, or even any thought of attack, on the person of the monarch, the father of all his peoples.

We have previously dealt with sexual and emotional self-divisions; these all are tributaries of the essential division that the theme of *parricide* turns up. Allusions to this theme multiply beginning with *The Landlady*. Murin, the enigmatic old man, rival of Ordynov, has murdered the parents of the young woman he has taken under his power. She is thus an accomplice. *Netotchka Nezvanova* (1849) seems particularly rich in psychopathological elements that are not mastered. The dream that ends one of the parts of the novel is an excellent text for noting how all the elements of the Dostoevskyan drama become interlaced.

At first it is the mother of Netotchka who plays the role of Dostoevsky's father. Netotchka does not love her, a woman rough and austere whose misfortunes have increased her sadness, but she adores her father, a violinist who is incapable and bohemian. The mother falls ill and dies of misery and exhaustion, but above all from lack of affection. Father and daughter flee together, like two accomplices, but then the father dies and Netotchka is taken in by some very rich people. Dreaming one night, she believes she hears anew the poignant and marvelous music that her father was playing the night her mother died. She opens a door and finds herself in an immense hall, luminous and warm, in the middle of a huge crowd gathered there to listen to the musician. Netotchka moves slowly toward the musician and he regards her with a smile; but the very moment he takes her into his arms she sees, struck with horror, that the man is not her father but his *double* and his assassin.

The entry into Belinsky's group was for Dostoevsky like entering into the concert hall for his heroine. But like Netotchka, his ecstasy was short-lived and was repaid twice over in anguish.

Less than a year after the final quarrel with Dostoevsky, Belinsky died. We do not know exactly when the epileptic or pseudo-epileptic seizures began from which the writer would have to suffer all his life. The first two of which we have an account took place, first, shortly after the murder of his father as he saw a funeral pass by, which probably recalled to the son the tragic event deeply buried in his memory; and second, upon the announcement of Belinsky's death.* The circle of failure that closes then upon Dostoevsky is thus, in its originary character, the circle of parricide. The writer is not completely wrong, perhaps, when he affirms that his four years of prison saved him from insanity.

There is something fateful about parricide. The young rebel becomes a vassal of Belinsky in order to rid himself of his father, but he falls again right away into the domain of the father and into parricide. Belinsky becomes the double of the father, Speshnev the *double* of Belinsky, etc. All the efforts to free himself only repeat and bind more tightly

*According to Joseph Frank, there is no evidence that Dostoevsky's genuine epileptic attacks began before 1850 when he was in prison. *Dostoevsky: The Years of Ordeal, 1850–1859* (Princeton: Princeton University Press, 1983), 77–81. This does not undercut the argument for a circle of parricide closing upon Dostoevsky, but it can no longer appeal to an early beginning of the epileptic episodes. — *Tr.*

the original cycle. To meditate on the relation of father and son is therefore to meditate, one time more, on the underground structure, on the relation to the hated rival who is equally the venerated model, but it enables apprehending this structure at a truly original level. There is not, therefore, a "theme of the father" which is added to previous themes; there is a reprise and deepening of all these themes. Here at last, at the most painful point, we reach the place that commands all the morbid manifestations, the object that all the underground mechanisms try to dissimulate.

❧

It is in *A Raw Youth** that the problem of the underground and the problem of the father begin to come together. Arkady, unacknowledged son of the nobleman Versilov and a servant woman, Sophie, suffers from not belonging, in a full legal sense, to the family of his father, but he is not able to reject the verdict that overwhelms him. Just as Dmitri, in *The Brothers Karamazov,* becomes the rival of his father with Grushenka, Arkady competes with Versilov over the object of his desires, the general's wife, Akhmakova; but it is not Akhmakova who constitutes what is really at stake in the rivalry, but the mother, Sophie, the *wisdom,* symbolically torn and divided by the underground conflict. The last dreams of the "life à trois" that the writer describes are also, and in every sense of the term, the first ones.

Bastardy is a legal and social consecration of a separation in union and a union in separation which characterizes the relation of father and son. Bastardy may therefore symbol-

---

*Known in English also as *The Adolescent* and *An Accidental Family.*

ize both this relation and the entire underground life that is the fruit of this relation. This symbol will be found in Sartre.

Depending on the circumstances or his humor of the moment, Versilov can act like a hero or a scoundrel. Arkady learns, for example, that he took up with a young woman, unknown and poor, who offered through advertisements in the newspapers to give private lessons of some sort. A little later the young woman hangs herself. Arkady, convinced of Versilov's perversity, refers to this affair in Versilov's presence, but Versilov, far from becoming disconcerted, deplores that the pride of the woman had prevented her from accepting his assistance. Arkady, who, held Versilov in utter contempt, begins to wonder whether he shouldn't admire him. His feelings for Versilov are always extreme. He certainly demonstrates underground ambivalence, but this ambivalence is justified in a way by the double nature of the father. Objective doubling, as always, confirms, encourages, and aggravates subjective doubling. The father, double character that he is, transmits his doubling to his son.

Versilov carries within him Myshkin and Stavrogin. These two characters, seen in the perspective of *A Raw Youth,* embody a new individualistic temptation, a new effort on the part of the writer to make one *part* of underground consciousness prevail to the exclusion of the other. *The Idiot* and *Demons* are not exempt from "Manicheanism" since Myshkin and Stavrogin have a separate existence, each in a different novel. In *A Raw Youth,* however, the two characters exist each only in function of the other, except from the point of view of Arkady who continually wonders whether his father is utterly good or utterly wicked. But the view of Arkady is precisely one that has no stability. The questions that Arkady poses to himself are those

that Dostoevsky was asking himself in his earlier works.
These questions are ones Dostoevsky no longer asks since
he answers them. In Versilov, Myshkin and Stavrogin are
juxtaposed; that is, Versilov is neither the one nor the other
of these two other characters. He is perhaps the victim of
the devil, but he is neither devil nor god. To the extent that
Dostoevsky climbs back into his own past, the illusory character of underground metaphysics is revealed in increasingly
better fashion.

In *A Raw Youth* Dostoevsky engages the problem of the
father but does not engage the problem of *his* father. As
concrete as this work may be in relation to the previous
ones, it remains abstract in relation to *The Brothers Karamazov.* Versilov is an aristocrat, an intellectual, someone
who prefers European culture. He represents again the Belinsky side of Dostoevsky's experience, an experience that
still remains divided at the primordial level. The other part,
the side of the father, is indeed present in *A Raw Youth,* but
in the idealized form of the *adoptive* father, Macar Dolgu-
ruky, the *wandering* mystic. There we find an inversion of
fathers and diverse "Manichean" phenomena of transposi-
tion which allow him to avoid the source of the problem
and which suggest the dreadful interior obstacles the writer
must yet confront.

The paternal aspect of the underground problem that is still
withdrawn in *A Raw Youth* moves to the foreground in *The
Brothers Karamazov.* This last novel, the masterwork of its
author, is based on the memory of Mikhail Andreevich Dostoevsky, the man assassinated by his serfs. The father of the
writer was very different from the old Karamazov in certain

respects. Never, for example, did he neglect the education of his children. So it is not that one must see in this sinister and repugnant old man a *portrait* of the father, and anyway, such a portrait would not have the same value as the creative work of the novelist. It is not the father *in and of himself*; it is the father *for the son* that this work reveals.

The rivalry of father and son implies a strict resemblance. The son desires what the father desires. The pride of the father thwarts the son and, in so doing, fortifies his pride in turn. Parricide, the crime of the son-slave committed against a tyrant father, thus comes into view as the underground tragedy par excellence. Because father and son are, in a sense, identical, parricide is simultaneously murder and suicide. In origin the two crimes are not differentiated. All the murders and all the suicides of the previously created heroes come together in this fundamental horror. The writer arrives at the source of all his nightmares.

At the source of the hatred of the Other there is the hatred of the Self. Beyond underground oppositions there is the identity that founds them, the identity of father and son. The father is hated as Other and, still more profoundly, he is the object of shame as Self. One senses this shame already prowling about Shatov in *Demons* and Arkady in *A Raw Youth,* but its precise object has eluded us every time. It is not until *The Brothers Karamazov* that this object truly appears and that shame loses, by the same stroke, its noxiousness. The basic but secret role that was propelling this emotion until now is going to disappear. Nothing will any longer bend Dostoevsky's work in the direction of derision and sarcasm.

The father as object of shame extends to the Russian tradition, to the national *being* itself. The first Dostoevsky gave

himself precipitously to Occidentalism in order to forget
his father and his paternal heritage. The Occidental attitude is associated with parricide, which is surely why the
later Dostoevsky will always see therein a veritable trea-
son. He believes he has discovered among the aristocrats
and reformist intellectuals a desire to forget the mores, culture, and language itself of Russia — a desire to get rid of
oneself, in short, in order to become Other. This mystical
desire obviously stems from underground idolatry, and it
is in Dostoevsky himself that it is most intense. The novelist "projects" his own feelings upon those around him
and transforms his obsessions into a universal system of
interpretation. That does not mean, of course, that his perspective is bad; perhaps he knew his contemporaries better
than they knew themselves. Is he not the person, indeed,
who pushes to extremes in his life what we ourselves would
dare to push only halfway?

Dostoevsky felt himself rejected by the advocates of European culture; he did not succeed in becoming one of them,
and he was not able to account himself as innocent. That
is why, after having denied guilt in rebellion, he let himself
come back to it and even be invaded by it. And then he
goes on to defend the paternal heritage with as much ardor
as devoted formerly to attacking it. But if he feels that the
peasant in himself directs his behavior from the moment he
enters the salon of Turgenev, he cannot contemplate an actual peasant without becoming again the person of the city,
the cosmopolitan intellectual that he swore not to be.

In the works of the Slavophil period, the resounding exaltation of all things Russian articulates what is really a
secret contempt. Misery, greed, disorder, and helplessness
are perceived as attributes of Russian existence, that is, of

the existence of Dostoevsky himself. In *The Gambler,* for instance, it can easily be confirmed that the deficiencies to which Dostoevsky attributes both his passion for gambling and the losses he suffers therein are those of the Russian people taken as a whole. Certain passages betray a "complex" much like one found among certain intellectuals of "third world" countries today:

> In the course of history the faculty to acquire capital has entered into the catechism of the virtue and merits of civilized European humans; perhaps it has even become the principal article of this catechism. Whereas Russians are not only incapable of acquiring capital, but squander it at random, without the least sense of propriety. However that may be, we Russians also need money.... Consequently, we are keen on methods such as roulette, at which one can make a fortune suddenly, in two hours, without working. That enraptures us, and as we play haphazardly, without taking pains of any sort, we lose.

The Europe-Russia opposition comes down to the difference of model-obstacle and disciple. The Dostoevsky of this period does not see that also in this sphere the difference is temporary, reversible, illusory. He tends, deeply within, to ascribe to it the fixity and rigidity of an *essence.* This Dostoevsky is neither reactionary nor Slavophil in a deep sense, just as the Dostoevsky of 1848 was not a revolutionary and Occidentalist. One should not confuse the writer, nor above all his genius, with the oscillations of the underground pendulum. This is precisely why all the interpretations that are based on ideology remain superficial, entrapped in the sterile oppositions produced by the conflict between the Other

and the Self. The double ideological extremism of Dostoevsky is an example of that *breadth* by which he himself
defines the modern individual.

Dostoevsky could not commit himself enduringly to anything. It is necessary to understand that all his commitments
are negatives. He is Russian, but this is against Europe; he is
proletarian, but this is against the rich; he is guilty, but this
is against the supposedly innocent. He is a stranger everywhere, stranger to Russian life from which his vocation as
intellectual and artist separates him, as well as the memory of his father; stranger to the cosmopolitan intelligentsia
that forms, with its rules and especially its prejudices, another society where the Turgenevs feel just as much at ease
as the peasants in their farm houses. But Dostoevsky himself feels at ease nowhere. In this regard the *utchitel* of *The
Gambler* is that one among his heroes whom he most resembles. This character is really doubly alienated, doubly
dispossessed. Feeling like an intellectual lackey of uprooted
aristocrats, he lives on the margins of a milieu that itself
exists on the margins of the national life.

Everywhere Feodor Mikhailovich feels himself excluded,
a pariah, the person no one ever invites, the one a host
would gladly cast outside if he had the misfortune to invite
him. It is not in doubt, moreover, that Dostoevsky did all
he could to give his hosts, particularly the most respectable
among them, an intense desire to eject him. Deeply within,
all these decisions to expel him, all the Siberias real and
imaginary, appear to him as perfectly justified, for his soul
remains submerged in shame and remorse.

Ashamed of being Russian, ashamed of being the son of
his father, ashamed of being Feodor Mikhailovich Dostoevsky, it is all this accumulated shame that is aired, ventilated,

and dissipated in the grand inspired breath of *The Brothers Karamazov.* For a person in love with truth, forgiveness and true absolution are incompatible with falsehood. It is because he did not dare, until now, really to look fully into the face of his father that he embraced him so tightly. Now he must regard everything; he must acknowledge to himself the guilt of the father after having acknowledged his own guilt; he must recognize that the unworthiness of the son as son is tied to the unworthiness of the father as father. He must, in short, write *The Brothers Karamazov.*

To desacralize the father is to triumph, finally, over abstract rebellion; it is to go beyond the false transcendence of Slavophil hysteria and reactionary frenzy. In his later years the attitude of the novelist toward Belinsky mellows considerably. All the critics have noted it, and they have noted equally a change in attitude toward Europe and reform movements. The conclusion has been that the later Dostoevsky starts a return to Occidentalism and to the ideas of his youth. But this is, perhaps, to regard these developments from the large end of the binoculars. The famous discourse on Pushkin is based entirely upon the idea of a synthesis between Slavophil and European currents, i.e., upon overcoming an opposition which is revealed to be secondary. That is certainly what the auditors of the two factions felt when they fell into the arms of one another, momentarily brought together by the eloquence of the orator. Pushkin, in this discourse, is presented as a truly universal artist, capable of reconciling in himself the genius of all the peoples. He is more Spanish than the Spanish, more English than the English, more German than the Germans. He becomes everything to everyone because he is really nothing; he is the universal artist, he is Dostoevsky himself, a Dostoevsky who is no longer overwhelmed with shame, but who in the end reclaims and assumes the inevitability of cultural alienation.

The objection will be made that this universality is presented as a specifically Russian phenomenon, so the overcoming of which we speak serves only to reenforce, after all, the panslavism of the writer. The fact is not to be denied, and we do not even consider denying it. There is, in the later Dostoevsky, a mixture of particularism and universalism that readers of the twentieth century can only regard with suspicion. But it is not the absolute value of the message that interests us, but the place where it occurs in the total evolution of the novelist. Everything indicates that he more and more renounces ideological modes of reflection. It is regrettable that this process of overcoming, still incomplete, results in formulations more disturbing, perhaps, than those of the strictly Slavophil period. It is all the more regrettable that the death of their author has had the effect of rendering these formulations definitive. But the fact itself of the renunciation of the Slavophil idea remains, and it is this alone that interests us.

Anyway, the political aspects of this last rupture are secondary, since it is politics, precisely, that Dostoevsky prepares to leave behind. All the self-divisions of underground pseudo-reflection are in the process of fading before the unity of a religious meditation come finally to its mature form.

What does the end of the revolt signify for Dostoevsky? Does it signify definitive and "sincere" adherence, this time, to the values of his father? Does Dostoevsky at last succeed at the point where he had previously failed? We believe, to the contrary, that Dostoevsky renounces the values of his father and all the other values which his pride has made into a weapon against the Other at any given moment of his existence. There cannot be a return of the prodigal son at the level of the earthly father. Rebellion is not bad because it rejects this or that value but because it is as little able to reject these values as to conserve them. Parricidal thought moves from antithesis to antithesis without ever advancing a step. Seeking the absolute Other, it falls back irresistibly into the Same. Rebellion is double, equivocal and diabolical, because it respects what it attacks and attacks what it respects. But it is good when it grapples with idols, even though it spends its power in a last and supreme idolatry. It is good not to be able to adhere to anything, not even to the Russian tradition, not even to the cosmopolitan intelligentsia. If the latter is insupportable it is not because it is culturally alienated, but because it is unfaithful, when all is said and done, to its calling of alienation; because, indeed, it finds again an appearance of stability in the heart of its contradictions, which should lead it to where they lead Dostoevsky himself: to a definitive rupture with cultural norms.

Rebellion is nonetheless bad, for it is incapable of pushing the alienation to the point of detachment, that is, to the freedom that comes from Christ and returns to him. Dostoevsky finally makes his way to this freedom with the aid of Christ in *The Brothers Karamazov,* and he celebrates it in the famous *Legend of the Grand Inquisitor.* It is put in the mouth of Ivan Karamazov as he seeks to explain to his brother Alyosha why he, Ivan, must "return his ticket" to a world which is not governed by a just and loving God — if there is a God.

࿔

The scene is in Seville in the end of the fifteenth century. Christ appears in a street and a crowd gathers about him, but the Grand Inquisitor comes along the way. He observes the mob and has Christ arrested. That night he goes to pay a visit to the prisoner in his dungeon and shows him, in a long discourse, the folly of his "idea."

> Thou wanted to found thy reign on that freedom that human beings hate and from which they always flee into some idolatry, even if they celebrate it with words. It would be better to make humans less free and thou hast made them more free, which only leads them to multiply their idols and conflicts between idols. Thou hast committed humanity to violence, misery, and disorder.

The Inquisitor predicts that a new Tower of Babel will be raised up, more dreadful than the former one and dedicated, like it, to destruction. The grand Promethean enterprise, fruit of Christian freedom, will end in "cannibalism."

The Grand Inquisitor is not unaware of anything that the underground, Stavrogin, and Kirillov have taught Dostoevsky. The vulgar rationalists find no trace of Christ, neither in the individual soul nor in history, but the Inquisitor asserts that the divine incarnation has made everything worse. The fifteen centuries gone by and the four centuries to come, whose course he prophesies, support his account.

The Inquisitor does not confuse the message of Christ with the psychological cancer to which it leads, by contrast to Nietzsche and Freud. He therefore doesn't accuse Christ of having underestimated human nature, but of having overestimated it, of not having understood that the impossible morality of love necessarily leads to a world of masochism and humiliation.

The Grand Inquisitor doesn't seek to make an end of idolatry by an act of metaphysical force, like Kirillov; he wants rather to heal evil with evil, to tie humans to immutable idols and, in particular, to an idolatrous conception of Christ. D. H. Lawrence, in a famous article, accused Dostoevsky of "perversity" because he placed in the mouth of a wicked inquisitor what he, Lawrence, regarded as the truth concerning human beings and the world.

The error of Christ, in the eyes of the Inquisitor, is all the less excusable because "he had adequate warnings." In the course of the temptations in the wilderness the devil, the "profound spirit of self-destruction and nothingness," revealed to the redeemer and placed at his disposal the three means capable of insuring the stability, well-being, and happiness of humanity. Christ disdained them, but the Inquisitor and his ilk have taken them up and work — always in the name of Christ but in a spirit contrary to his — for the advent of an earthly kingdom more in keeping with the limitations of human nature.

Agreeing with Dostoevsky, Simone Weil saw in the inquisition the archetype of all totalitarian solutions. The end of the Middle Ages is an essential moment in Christian history; the heir, having reached the age of an adult, lays claim to his heritage. His guardians are not wrong to mistrust his maturity, but they are wrong to want to prolong indefinitely their tutelage. The Legend resumes the problem of evil at the precise point where *Demons* abandoned it. The underground appeared in this novel as the failure and reversal of Christianity. The wisdom of the redeemer, and especially his redemptive power, are notably absent. Rather than hide his

own anxiety from himself, Dostoevsky expresses it and gives
it an extraordinary fulness. He never combats nihilism by
fleeing from it.

Christianity disappointed Dostoevsky. Christ himself has
surely not responded to his expectation. There is, in the first
place, the misery that he has not abolished, then the suffering, and also the daily bread that he has not given to all
human beings. He has not "changed life." That is the first
reproach, and the second is yet more serious. Christianity
does not bring certitude; why does God not send a proof
of his existence, a *sign,* to those who would believe in him,
but don't attain this belief? And finally and above all, there
is that pride which no effort, no prostration of oneself is
able to reduce, that pride which goes as far, sometimes, as
envying Christ himself....

When he defines his own grievances against Christianity,
Dostoevsky encounters the Gospel, he encounters the three
"temptations in the wilderness":

Then Jesus was led by the Spirit out into the wilderness
to be tempted by the devil. He fasted for forty days
and forty nights, after which he was very hungry, and
the tempter came and said to him, "If thou art the Son
of God, tell these stones to turn into loaves." But he
replied, "Scripture says:

Man does not live on bread alone
but on every word that comes from the mouth
of God."

The devil then took him to the holy city and made
him stand on the parapet of the Temple. "If thou art

the Son of God," he said, "throw thyself down; for Scripture says:

> He will put thee in his angels' charge,
> and they will support thee on their hands
> in case thou hurtest thy foot against a stone."

Jesus said to him, "Scripture also says:

> Thou must not put the Lord your God to the test."

Next, taking him to a very high mountain, the devil showed him all the kingdoms of the world and their splendor. "I will give thee all these," he said, "if thou fallest at my feet and worship me." Then Jesus replied, "Be off, Satan! For Scripture says:

> Thou shalt worship the Lord thy God,
> and serve him alone."

Then the devil left him, and angels appeared and looked after him.

(Matthew 4:1–11)*

These are indeed the major temptations of Dostoevsky: social messianism, doubt, and pride. The last one is especially worthy of meditation. Everything that the proud desire leads them, after all, to prostrate themselves before the *Other*, Satan. The only moments of his life when Feodor Mikhailovich did not succumb to one or the other of the temptations were those when he succumbed to all three at

---

*The translation of Gospel passages follows the Jerusalem Bible except for the use of the archaic pronouns "thou," "thy," "thee." Dostoevsky evidently made the language of the Inquisitor archaic, and this pronoun usage helps to convey that. — *Tr.*

´once. So it is therefore to himself in particular that this
message is addressed; the Legend is the proof that he finally understands its call. The presence in the Gospel of
Matthew of a text so adapted to his needs affords him
great comfort. There it is, the sign he was seeking, as he
tells us in brilliant and veiled fashion by the mouth of his
Inquisitor:

And could one say anything more penetrating than
what was said to thee in the three questions or, to
speak in the language of the Scriptures, the "temptations" that thou rejected? If ever there had been on
earth an authentic and resounding miracle, it occurred
the day of the three temptations. The very formulation of these three questions constitutes a miracle. Let
us suppose that they had disappeared from the Scriptures, that it had been necessary to compose them, to
imagine them anew in order to replace them there, and
that one had gathered for this all the sages of the earth,
persons of state, prelates, scholars, philosophers, poets,
saying to them: imagine and compose three questions
which not only correspond to the importance of that
event, but express in three sentences all the history of
future humanity — dost thou believe that this summit
gathering of human wisdom could imagine anything as
strong and profound as the three questions put to thee
by the powerful Spirit? These three questions prove,
all by themselves, that one has met here the eternal
and absolute Spirit and not a transitory human mind.
For they summarize and predict simultaneously all the
later history of humanity. These are the three forms in
which all the insoluble contradictions of human nature

are crystalized. One could not understand it then, for
the future was veiled, but now, after fifteen centuries
have elapsed, we see that everything had been foreseen
in these three questions and has been realized to the
point that it is impossible to add anything to them or
to remove a single word from them.

The Legend is basically only the repetition and expan-
sion of the Gospel scene evoked by the Grand Inquisitor.
This is what must be understood when one wonders, a little
naively, about the silence that Alyosha maintains in face of
the arguments of this new tempter. There is no "refuting"
of the Legend since, from a Christian point of view, it is the
devil, it is the Grand Inquisitor, it is Ivan who is right. The
world is delivered over to evil. In St. Luke the devil asserts
that every earthly power has been delivered to him "and I
give it to whom I will." Christ does not "refute" this assertion. Never does he speak in his own name; he takes refuge
behind the citations of Scripture. Like Alyosha, he refuses
to debate.
The Grand Inquisitor believes he can praise Satan, but it
is of the Gospel that he speaks, it is the Gospel that has pre-
served its freshness after fifteen, after nineteen centuries of
Christianity. And it is not only in the instance of the temptations, but at each moment the Legend echoes the Gospel
sayings:

Do not suppose that I have come to bring peace to
the earth: it is not peace I have come to bring but a
sword. For I have come to set a man against his father,
a daughter against her mother. . . .

(Matthew 10:34–35a)

The central idea of the Legend, that of the risk entailed by the increase of freedom for humans, or of the grace conferred by Christ, a risk the Grand Inquisitor refuses to run — this very idea figures in passages of the Gospel which evoke irresistibly Dostoevsky's concept of underground metaphysics.

When an unclean spirit goes out of a man it wanders through waterless country looking for a place to rest, and cannot find one. Then it says, "I will return to the house I came from." But on arrival, finding it unoccupied, swept, and tidied, it then goes off and collects seven other spirits more evil than itself, and they go in and set up house there, so that the man ends up by being worse than he was before. That is what will happen to this evil generation.

(Matthew 12:43–45)

Behind the dark pessimism of the Grand Inquisitor is the outline of an eschatological vision of history that responds to the question *Demons* left in suspense. Because he foresaw the rebellion of man, Christ foresaw also the sufferings and ruptures that his coming would cause. The proud assurance of the orator allows us to discern a new paradox, that of the divine Providence which effortlessly outwits the calculations of rebellion. The reappearance of Satan does not nullify his prior defeat. Everything must finally converge toward the good, even idolatry.

If the world flees Christ, he will be able to make this flight serve his redemptive plan. In division and contradiction he will accomplish what he wanted to accomplish in union and joy. In seeking to divinize itself without Christ, humankind places itself on the cross. It is the freedom of

Christ, perverted but still vital, that produces the underground. There is not a fragment of human nature that is not
kneaded and pressed in the conflict between the Other and
the Self. Satan, divided against himself, expels Satan. The
idols destroy the idols. Humankind exhausts, little by little,
all illusions, including inferior notions of God swept away
by atheism. It is caught in a vortex more and more rapid as
its always more frantic and mendacious universe strikingly
reveals the absence and need of God. The prodigious series
of historical catastrophes, the improbable cascade of em-
pires and kingdoms, of social, philosophical, and political
systems that we call Western civilization, the circle always
greater which covers over an abyss at whose heart history
collapses ever more speedily — all this accomplishes the plan
of divine redemption. It is not the plan that Christ would
have chosen for human beings if he had not respected their
freedom, but the one they have chosen for themselves in
rejecting him.

Dostoevsky's art is literally prophetic. He is not prophetic
in the sense of predicting the future, but in a truly biblical
sense, for he untiringly denounces the fall of the people of
God back into idolatry. He reveals the exile, the rupture,
and the suffering that results from this idolatry. In a world
where the love of Christ and the love of the neighbor form
one love, the true touchstone is our relation to others. It
is the Other whom one must love *as oneself* if one does
not desire to idolize and hate the Other in the depths of
the underground. It is no longer the golden calf, it is this
Other who poses the risk of seducing humans in a world
committed to the Spirit, for better or for worse.

Between the two forms of idolatry, the one attacked in the
Old Testament and the other unmasked in the New, there

are the same differences and the same analogical relation as between the rigidity of the law and universal Christian freedom. All the biblical words that describe the first idolatry describe analogously the second. This is certainly why the prophetic literature of the Old Testament has remained fresh and alive.

The Christianity that the Inquisitor describes is like the negative of a photograph — it shows everything in a reversed manner, just like the words of Satan in the account of the temptations. It has nothing to do with the metaphysical milk toast that a certain bourgeois piety holds up as a mirror to itself. Christ wanted to make humans into superhumans, but by means opposed to those of Promethean thought. So the arguments of the Grand Inquisitor are turned against him when one understands them as they are intended. It is just this that the pure Alyosha observes to his brother Ivan, the author and narrator of the Legend. "Everything that you say serves not to blame, but to praise Christ."

Christ has been voluntarily deprived of all prestige and all power. He refuses to exercise the least pressure; he desires to be loved for himself. To reiterate, it is here the Inquisitor who speaks. What Christian would want to "refute" such statements? The Inquisitor sees all, knows all, understands all. He understands even the mute appeal of love but is incapable of responding to it. What to do in this case but to reaffirm the presence of this love? Such is the sense of the kiss that Christ gives, wordlessly, to the wretched old man. Alyosha, too, kisses his brother at the conclusion of his story and Ivan accuses him, laughingly, of plagiary.

❧

The diabolical choice of the Inquisitor is nothing else than a reflection of the diabolical choice made by Ivan Karamazov. The four brothers are accomplices in the murder of their father, but the guiltiest of all is Ivan, for he is the one who inspires the act of murder. The bastard Smerdyakov is the double of Ivan, whom he admires and hates passionately. To kill the father in place of Ivan is to put into practice the audacious statements of this master of rebellion; it is to anticipate his most secret desires; it is to go even further on the road he himself designated. But a diabolical double is soon substituted beside Ivan for this double who is still human.

The hallucination of the double synthesizes, as we have seen, quite a series of subjective and objective phenomena belonging to underground existence. This hallucination, at once true and false, is not perceived until the phenomenon of doubling reaches a certain degree of intensity and gravity.

The hallucination of the devil that Ivan experiences may be explicated, at the phenomenal level, by a *new aggravation* of psychopathological troubles produced by pride; it embodies, on the religious level, the metaphysical overcoming of underground psychology. The more one approaches madness, the more one equally approaches the truth, and if one does not fall into the former, one must end up necessarily in the latter.

What is the traditional conception of the devil? This character is the father of lies; he is thus simultaneously true and false, illusory and real, fantastic and everyday. Outside of us when we believe him to be in us, he is in us when we believe him outside of us. Although he leads an existence useless and parasitic, he is morally and resolutely "Manichean." He offers us a grimacing caricature of what is worst in us. He is at once both seducer and adversary. He does not cease to thwart the desires that he suggests and if, by chance, he satisfies them it is in order to deceive us.

It is superfluous to emphasize the relations between this devil and the Dostoevskyan double. The individuality of the devil, like that of the double, is not a point of departure, but an outcome. Just as the double is the origin of all doublings or divisions, the devil is the locus and the origin of all possessions and other demoniacal manifestations. The objective reading of the underground leads to demonology. And there is no reason to by astonished by that, for we are really always in this "kingdom of Satan" which is not able to maintain itself, for "it is *divided* against itself."

Between the double and the devil there is not a relation of identity but a relation of analogy. One moves from the first to the second in the way in which one moves from the portrait to the caricature; the caricaturist relies on characteristic features and suppresses those that are not. The devil, parodist par excellence, is himself the fruit of parody. For an artist imitates himself, he simplifies, schematizes, makes himself starker in his own essence, in order finally to render ever more striking the meanings with which his work is permeated.

There is no break in continuity, no metaphysical *leap* between the double and the devil. One moves imperceptibly from one to the other, just as one passed imperceptibly from romantic doublings to the personified double. The process is essentially *aesthetic*. For Dostoevsky there is, as for most great artists, what could be called an "operational formalism," from which, however, a formalist theory of art should not be deduced. Perhaps the distinction between form and content, which is always dialectical, is not truly legitimate except from the standpoint of the creative process. It is proper to define the artist by his quest for form, because by form as intermediary he accomplishes the penetration of reality, the knowledge of the world and himself. The form here literally precedes the meaning, and this is why it is bestowed as "pure" form.

In Dostoevsky the devil is thus called forth by an irresistible tendency to bring forth the structure of some fundamental obsessions which constitute the primary subject-matter of the work. The idea of the devil does not introduce any new element, but it organizes the old ones in a more coherent and meaningful manner. In fact, this idea is revealed as the only one capable of unifying all the phenomena observed. There is not a gratuitous intervention of the supernatural in the natural world. The devil is not represented to us as the *cause* of the phenomena. For example, he repeats all the ideas of Ivan, who recognizes in him a "projection" of his sick brain but who ends up, like Luther, by throwing an inkwell at his head.

Ivan's devil is even more interesting to the extent that Dostoevsky's realism is so scrupulous. Never, before *The Brothers Karamazov,* had the theme of the devil contaminated that of the double. Even in the "romantic" period we do not find in Dostoevsky those purely literary and decorative comparisons and connections to which the German writers devote themselves so readily. On the other hand, he had already thought about giving a satanic double to the persona of Stavrogin, but this double is already that of Ivan. It is particularly with *Demons,* one may recall, that the entire underground psychology appears to Dostoevsky as an inverted image of the Christian structure of reality, as precisely its *double.* If Dostoevsky temporarily withdrew from his idea, it was not because the novelist within him still held in check a fanaticism to which he gave free rein in *The Brothers Karamazov*. It is rather because he feared misunderstanding from the public. The interior demand and motivation were not yet mature enough to surmount this obstacle.

With *The Brothers Karamazov* all things are accomplished. The devil is totally objectified, expelled, exorcised; he must therefore figure in the work as the devil as such. Pure evil is disengaged, and its nothingness is revealed. It no longer causes fear, for separated from the being that it haunts, it seems even derisory and ridiculous, nothing more than a bad nightmare.

This impotence of the devil is not a gratuitous idea, but a truth inscribed on all the pages of the work. If the Inquisitor is able to express only what is good, this is because he goes further in evil than all his predecessors. There is almost no longer any difference between his reality and that of the elect. Indeed, it is with full knowledge that he chooses evil. Almost everything he says is true, but his conclusions are radically false. The last words he states are the pure and simple inversion of the words that end the New Testament in the Apocalypse: for the *marana tha* of the early Christians — "Come, O Lord" — he substitutes a diabolic "Don't come back, don't ever come back, ever!"

This evil that is at once the strongest and the feeblest is evil seized at its root, that is, evil revealed as pure *choice*. The pinnacle of diabolic lucidity is also extreme blindness. The Dostoevsky of *The Brothers Karamazov* is just as ambiguous as the romantic Dostoevsky, but the terms of ambiguity are no longer the same. In *The Insulted and Injured* the rhetoric of altruism, nobility, and devotion covers over pride, masochism, and hate. In *The Brothers Kara-*

mazov it is pride that comes into the foreground. But the frenzied discourses of this pride allow us to catch a glimpse of a good that has nothing otherwise in common with romantic rhetoric.

Dostoevsky lets evil speak to bring it to the point where it refutes and condemns itself. The Inquisitor discloses his scorn for humanity and his appetite for domination that drives him to prostrate himself before Satan. But this self-refutation, the self-destruction of evil must not be utterly explicit for otherwise it would lose all its aesthetic and spiritual value. It would lose, in other words, its value as *temptation.* This art of which the Legend is the model could indeed be defined as the art of temptation. All the characters of the novel, or almost all, are tempters of Alyosha: his father, his brothers, and also Grushenka, the seductress, who gives money to the wicked monk Rakitin so that he will lead Alyosha to her. Father Zossima himself becomes, after his death, the object of a new temptation as the rapid decomposition of his corpse shocks the naive faith of the monastic community.

But the most terrible tempter is certainly Ivan when he presents the suffering of innocent children as a motif of metaphysical revolt. Alyosha is stunned and upset, but the tempter, once again, is powerless, for without knowing it he works even for the victory of the good, since he incites his brother to concern himself with the unfortunate little Ilyusha and his friends. The same reasons that distance the rebel from Christ impel those open to love toward him. Alyosha well knows that the pain he experiences at the thought of the suffering children comes from Christ himself.

Between the temptations of Christ and the temptations of Alyosha there is an analogy that underlines the parallelism of the two kisses given to the two tempters. The Legend is presented as a series of concentric circles around the Gospel archetype: circle of the Legend, circle of Alyosha, and finally the circle of the readers themselves. The art of the tempter-novelist consists in revealing, behind all human situations, the choices that they imply. The novelist is not the devil but his advocate, *advocatus diaboli*. He preaches the false in order to lead us to what is true. The task of the reader consists in recognizing, with Alyosha, that everything he has just read "is not for the blame but the praise of Christ."

The Slavophil and reactionary friends of Dostoevsky did not recognize anything at all. No one, it seems, was really ready for an art so simple and so great. They expected of a Christian novelist some reassuring formulas, some simplistic distinctions between good and bad people, in a word, "religious" art in the ideological sense. The art of the later Dostoevsky is terribly ambiguous from the point of view of the sterile oppositions with which the world is filled because it is terribly clear from the spiritual point of view. Constantine Pobedonostzev, the procurator of the Holy Synod, was the first to demand this "refutation," whose absence continues to chagrin or elate so many contemporary critics. There is no need to be astonished if Dostoevsky himself ratifies, in a way, this superficial reading of his work by promising the demanded refutation. It is not the author but the reader who defines the objective meaning of the work. If the reader does not perceive that the strongest negation affirms, how would the writer know that this affirmation is really present in his text? If the reader does not perceive that rebellion and adoration finally converge, how would the writer know that this convergence is effectively realized? How could he analyze the art which he is in the process of living? How would he divine that it is the reader, not he, who is wrong? He knows the spirit in which he has written his work, but the results escape him. If one says to him that the effect sought is not visible, he can only bow. This is why Dostoevsky promises to refute the irrefutable without ever following through, and this for good reason.

The pages devoted to the death of Father Zossima are beautiful, but they do not have the force of genius found in the invectives of Ivan. The critics who try to bend Dostoevsky in the direction of atheism insist on the laborious character that Dostoevsky's positive expression of the good always had. The observation is fair, but the conclusions usually drawn from it are not. Those who demand of Dostoevsky a "positive" art see in this art solely the adequate expression of Christian faith. But these are always people who conceive a lame idea either of art or of Christianity. The art of extreme negation is perhaps, to the contrary, the only Christian art adapted to our time, the only art worthy of it. This art does not require listening to sermons, for our era cannot tolerate them. It lays aside traditional metaphysics, with which nobody, or almost nobody, can comply. Nor does it base itself on reassuring lies, but on consciousness of universal idolatry.

Direct assertion and affirmation is ineffective in contemporary art, for it necessarily invokes intolerable chatter about Christian *values*. The Legend of the Grand Inquisitor escapes from shameful nihilism and the disgusting insipidity of values. The art that emerges in its entirety from the miserable and splendid existence of the writer seeks affirmation beyond negations. Dostoevsky does not claim to escape from the underground. To the contrary, he plunges into it so profoundly that his light comes to him from the other side. "It is not as a child that I believe in Christ and confess him. It is through the crucible of doubt that my Hosanna has passed."

❧

This art that reveals in broad daylight the divisions and doublings of idolatrous pride is no longer itself divided. To say that it reveals good and evil as pure choice is to say that no Manicheanism remains in it. We feel that at any moment Ivan might save himself and Alyosha could be lost. The purity of the latter, always endangered, has nothing to do with the unchangeable perfection of a Myshkin. There are no longer righteous and wicked characters *in themselves*. There is no longer but one sole human reality. Here we have the supreme form of art "by gathering." Good and evil here become alternating voices in the same choir. However ferocious their combat, it can no longer harm the harmony of the whole. The great scenes of the novel are so many fragments of a veritable Christian epic.

The works about underground life transpire frequently, as we have seen, in weather of fog or of snow mixed with rain. This equivocal and indistinct weather of the season in between, the weather divided against itself, as it were, makes way in many scenes of *The Brothers Karamazov* and especially in the episodes of childhood, for wind, sun, icy cold, and sparkling snow of real winter days. The pure light restores clarity and identity to all objects and the ice tightens and contracts everything. This healthy and cheerful weather is the weather of the oneness finally conquered and possessed.

The richness and diversity of the work makes this unity particularly remarkable. It may be better judged if one con-

siders that the scientific disciplines which deal with the
material of the novel are unable to reconcile their discoveries. The sociologists, for example, will recognize in
underground idolatry a form of fetishism which informs social structures left behind by historical evolution. They will
want to account for the novelistic data by the fact that
the Karamazovs belong to a feudal society at the point of
complete disintegration. The psychoanalysts will ascribe this
same idolatry to the "Oedipus" conflict. Sociologists and
psychoanalysts fiercely close the circle of their descriptions.
They know only a narrow segment arbitrarily cut out of social reality, and they want always to determine the causes at
the same level as the phenomena observed.

Dostoevsky shows us that in the corrupt society of the
Karamazovs the serfs are not treated like children, but the
children are often treated like serfs. He shows us how individuals, traumatized in their early infancy, imprint the most
diverse situations with irrational imaginings, transforming
each one of them into a repetition of the initial trauma.
And he shows us, finally, the perpetual overlapping of individual behavior and collective structures. The novelist is
an excellent sociologist and psychiatrist. But these two tal-
ents are not contradictions in his thought and work. The
dynamic of events is never interrupted by a cause or a system of causes. The God of Alyosha is not a cause; he is an
opening to the world and to the Other. And because the
novelist never closes the circle of the observation of events,
his power of evocation is prodigious.

At the heart of everything there is always human pride
or God, that is, the two forms of freedom. It is pride that
maintains troubling memories deeply concealed; it is pride
that separates us from ourselves and others. Individual neu-

roses and oppressive social structures stem essentially from
pride hardened and petrified. To become aware of pride and
its dialectic is to renounce the cutting up of reality and to
rise above the division of particular branches of knowledge
toward the unity of a religious vision, the only vision that
is universal.

But to master this dialectic something other than intelligence is required. It requires a victory over pride itself. The
proud intellect will never comprehend the saying of Christ:
"Whoever does not gather with me scatters." Pride goes always toward dispersion and final division, which is to say,
toward death. But to accept this death is to be reborn into
unity. The work that gathers in place of scattering, the work
that is truly one, will thus itself have the form of death and
resurrection, i.e., the form of victory over pride.

The double expelled and unity recovered, these are the
romantic angel and beast that vanish to make way for the
human being in his integrity. Honest reason and true realism
triumph over the chimeras of the underground. In coming
to regard himself first of all as a sinner, the writer is not di-
verted from what is concrete nor is he submerged in morbid
delight; he opens himself rather to a spiritual experience for
which his work is at once the recompense and witness.

This experience does not differ essentially from that of
Saint Augustine or Dante. This is why the structure of *The
Brothers Karamazov* is close to the form of *The Confessions*
and *The Divine Comedy*. It is the structure of the incarnation, the fundamental structure of Western art and Western
experience. It is present every time artists succeed in giving their work the *form* of the spiritual metamorphosis that
brings the work to birth. It is not the same as the narration
of this metamorphosis, even though it may coincide with it;

it is not always completed in the religious conversion that its full blossoming would demand. If we take a last look at the work of Dostoevsky in light of *The Brothers Karamazov,* we will confirm that this form, perfect as it is in this last novel, does not first appear with it but has been a matter of slow maturation.

This form appears for the first time in the conclusion of *Crime and Punishment;* it is once again absent from *The Idiot,* a work which bears traces of romantic angelism, but it is reaffirmed in *Demons* with the death of Stepan Trofi-movitch, which is a spiritual healing. In *A Raw Youth* the hero, Arkady, becomes aware, little by little, of the inferno in which he is submerged and, because of this, he extricates himself. The underground no longer appears as an almost irreversible condition but as a transition. The hate that it in-spires vanishes with it, for this hate is itself an underground condition. But the form of the incarnation does not open into full expression in this novel as it does, finally, in *The Brothers Karamazov,* where it is no longer limited to one character and now becomes identical with the work itself.

This form thus has a history and this history coincides with the stages of a spiritual healing. It cannot come to birth except when the novelist begins to emerge from the under-ground. It cannot attain its full development except with full freedom. The entire "romantic" period thus presents itself, retrospectively, as a descent into hell, and the Dostoevsky of *The Insulted and Injured* seems to invite the question of Alyosha concerning his brother Ivan: "Either he will be res-urrected into the light of truth or he will perish from hate." That is, not only the particular works in light of *The Broth-ers Karamazov,* but the entire oeuvre and the very existence of the novelist have the form of a death and a resurrection.

And the last novel takes up everything again, summarizes
everything, concludes everything, for it alone embodies the
fulness of this resurrection. Because the spiritual exhorta-
tions of Zossima convey to us the religious experience of
Dostoevsky, they convey equally his aesthetics, his vision of
history, and the profound meaning of his life.

> What you think is bad in you is purified for the sole
> reason that you yourself have detected it.... At the mo-
> ment you come to see in fear that, despite your efforts,
> you not only have not come nearer to the goal, but
> are even further away than before — at that very mo-
> ment I predict that you will attain the goal and you will
> see above you the mysterious power of the Lord who,
> unknown to you, has guided you with love.

Mimetic Desire
in the Underground

by René Girard

I am grateful to my good friend James Williams for translating and editing with great care the foregoing essay on Dostoevsky. When I wrote it I had just published the original French version of a longer book on five European novelists, including Dostoevsky. In that book, *Deceit, Desire and the Novel,* the chief principle of interpretation is the idea of *mimetic desire,* which emerged from its creation and which has dominated my work ever since.

The present book relies on mimetic desire, therefore, but not in very explicit fashion. In order to fit the original publisher's requirements, I had to keep it short and I did not want to reformulate in such limited space the theoretical apparatus elaborated at length only a short time before. I was afraid it would seem repetitious and cumbersome. As a result the essay sounds more impressionistic than it really is.

I would be well advised, perhaps, to perpetuate this illusion. Mimetic desire is often regarded as an artificial construct, a "reductionist" device that impoverishes the literary works to which it is "applied." During my entire

143

career, the "reductionist" objection has dogged my books
with the regularity of a Pavlovian reflex and if there is a
chance to escape unscathed for a change, why spoil it?

Mimetic desire is "reductionist," no doubt, but so is the
very process of abstraction, and, unless we renounce thinking altogether, we cannot give up abstracting. Even if it were
a viable option, a non-reductionist interpretation would
merely paraphrase Dostoevsky; it would be of no interest
to me. The only concrete choice, I feel, is between good and
bad reductionism.

Since our starting point is mimetic desire, we must begin
with its definition. To say that our desires are imitative or
mimetic is to root them neither in their objects nor in ourselves but in a third party, the *model* or *mediator,* whose
desire we imitate in the hope of resembling him or her,
in the hope that our two beings will be "fused," as some
Dostoevskyan characters love to say.

The psychologists interested in *role models* tell us that
young people, when they grow up, must imitate the best
possible models. These should be older persons who have
made a place for themselves in the community. If the growing youngsters imitate these good people, presumably they
will not go astray.

What I like about the idea of role model is the paramount
function that, at least implicitly, it attributes to imitation.
Most psychologists believe, mistakenly in my view, that imitation affects only our superficial attitudes and manners. If it
did not influence our very *desires,* even the best role models
could have no significant influence on their imitators.

Why do peers, as a rule, even if not intrinsically bad,
make bad role models? As I borrow the desire of a model
from whom nothing separates me, neither time and space,

nor prestige and social hierarchy, we both inevitably desire the same object and, unless this object can be shared and we are willing to share it, we will compete for it. Instead of uniting us, our shared desire will turn us into rivals and potential enemies.

This *mimetic rivalry* is most obvious in small children. When two of them are left to play together, even and especially on a mountain of toys, the togetherness does not last. As soon as one child selects a toy, the other tries to take it away from him.

The second child imitates the first. And the first child does his utmost to retain possession of the toy, not because this one, at least, "knows what he or she wants," but for the opposite reason. The first child does not know any better than the second, and the latter's interference reinforces the original choice. Conflicts of desire keep occurring not because strongly individualized desires strongly oppose one another but for the opposite reason. Each child takes the other as the model and guide of a desire that must be fundamentally free-floating and unattached since it attaches itself most stubbornly to the object of its rival, not only in children but in adults as well.

Because of their mimetic nature, the rivalries of desires keep escalating, and the disputed objects acquire more and more value in the eyes of both rivals, even if the initial choice had no significance whatever, even if it was more or less random.

We hate to think that adults behave like children in matters of desire, especially in an "individualistic" world such as ours, but we do. We all protest that our desires are strictly our own, and we despise imitation, but we imitate one another more fiercely than children. The only difference is that, unlike children, we are ashamed and we try to hide our imitation.

When we borrow the desires of those we admire we must play the deadly serious game of mimetic rivalry with them. Whenever we lose, our models successfully thwart our desires and, because we admire them, we feel rejected and humiliated. But since their victory over us confirms their superiority we admire them more than ever and our desire becomes more intense.

As our confidence in our models increases, our self-confidence decreases. When this frustration occurs too often, and we turn too many models into rivals and obstacles, our perversely logical mind tends to speed up the process and automatically turn obstacles into models. We become *obstacle addicts,* so to speak, unable to desire in the absence of a an-obstacle-who-is-also-a-model, a beloved enemy who has "turned a heaven into a hell" (*A Midsummer Night's Dream,* 1, 1, 207)

What does all this have to do with Dostoevsky? Everything. Take the "hero" of *Notes from the Underground:* this puny little man, this "acutely conscious mouse," entirely devoid of charisma, always finds himself in the most grotesque situations. One day, in a billiard room, he stands in the way of some arrogant petty officer who, most unceremoniously, lifts him from one spot and puts him down in another.

Because the officer treats him as an insignificant obstacle, our hero sees him as an enormous, a monstrous obstacle that must be overturned at all cost. This we can well understand. What seems inexplicable, however, is that, simultaneously, he sees the officer as a fascinating idol with whom he would like to be "fused."

The officer is automatically transformed into a model

simply because he is an infuriating obstacle. The underground man spends long hours trying to fulfill his twofold desires — overturning the obstacle and becoming "fused" with it — into an appropriate revenge which finally consists in — what else? — mimicking his insultor and treating him as an insignificant obstacle himself, jostling him off the sidewalk on the famous Nevsky Prospekt, the elegant promenade of St. Petersburg.

Childish rivalries are quickly extinguished and forgotten. ... Adult rivalries go on forever and have a lasting influence. When physical violence is suppressed, as normally happens in modern civilized life, all frustrated rivalries go underground and show up as "psychopathological symptoms," the very symptoms exhibited by underground characters in Dostoevsky's masterpieces.

One goes "underground" as a result of frustrated mimetic desire. All underground people carefully hide their imitations, even from themselves, so as not to give their models the psychic reward of seeing themselves imitated, not to humiliate themselves by being revealed as imitators.

Dostoevsky grants a quasi-technical value to the word *underground*. He used it again in *The Eternal Husband*, in connection with the "apishness" of his central character, who is another, slightly different type of underground "anti-hero."

For many years, his wife was having love affairs on a regular basis. After her premature death, the widower leaves his provincial town for Petersburg, in search of her former lovers, and he keeps circling around one of these who is also the narrator of our story. For many a day this behavior remains enigmatic.

Our culture is so steeped in psychoanalytical lore that

most of us, when asked to solve this enigma, suggest that
the eternal husband must be "unconsciously" in love with
his rival. This is Freud's "latent homosexuality" hypothesis.
In our particular case, it was proposed by the master himself in his article on Dostoevsky. The difficulty with it is that
it leaves 95 percent of the story out of account.

Mimetic desire works better. Quite understandably, the
eternal husband feels deficient in the art of seduction. To
remedy his inferiority, he seeks the best possible model and,
from his own personal standpoint, it has to be the man who
supplanted him in the heart of his wife, demonstrating *ipso
facto* his superior expertise in the erotic field. This choice is
startling not because it is irrational but because it is based
on an unimpeachable logic.

The true nature of the relationship becomes obvious
when the eternal husband decides to marry again and invites his former rival to come along for a visit to his
prospective bride.

He pictures himself as a modern man, an "individualist,"
and he has chosen his future wife independently from his
model, but then he cannot go ahead with his project unless
the eternal lover approves of his choice. The young woman
must be stamped with the latter's official seal, so to speak.

The eternal husband expects and even hopes, yes, he
hopes that the eternal lover will find his prospective wife
desirable, that he will actually desire her. Without this guarantee of quality, she would not seem worth marrying and
the eternal husband would look for a better prospect, more
to the liking of his model.

At first, the eternal lover is scandalized at the idea of
meeting the girl, but the invitation is repeated and he
feels a mysterious compulsion to accept. She is ludicrously

young but, as soon as he is introduced to her, the eternal lover starts acting as if he, too, were interested in her and, very quickly, between the two a semi-erotic complicity is established, against her ridiculous suitor, the eternal husband.

At first, we believe that the latter has willfully engineered this new humiliation, but, on closer examination, we can see that he is looking forward to more mimetic rivalry with the eternal lover, which he hopes to win this time. The eternal lover responds in kind; his competitive urge is aroused. The two men behave like two children fighting over the same toy.

The eternal husband is in love not with his rival but with his rival's *success as a lover.* Like a bold gambler, he wants to recoup his losses at one single stroke. The only triumph that really interests him is the one he would achieve at the expense of his rival.... He will never achieve it. Being less elegant and handsome than the eternal lover, he will always come out second best. His frantic desire for *revanche* exposes him to endless defeats. The eternal lover's successes and the eternal husband's failures are the two sides of the same coin.

And yet the relationship is less one-sided than it seems. The two men interchange their roles in the one case of poor little Liza, the adulterous wife's daughter, who may also be the eternal lover's daughter.... The eternal husband cruelly uses her to blackmail his revered enemy. And yet Liza dearly loves and pities the man whom she regards as her real father, rightly surmising that he has been greatly wronged and he greatly suffers. When the eternal lover takes her away from the eternal husband, she becomes ill and she dies.

Since the objects of our desires are infinitely diverse and

forever changing, when we try to understand desire in general, we must avoid the mistake of Marx, Freud, and others, and we must privilege no particular category of objects. Desire can be understood neither through its objects nor through its subjects. We must interpret many phenomena through the human subject, such as appetites and needs on the one hand, disinterested affection on the other, and all these things can get mixed with desire, no doubt, but desire as such is something else. What we must stress is the convergence of two or several desires on the same object which may increase enormously the value of literally any object. Mimetic desire is a realistic theory of why human beings cannot be realists.

∾

In the first and more theoretical part of *Notes from the Underground,* the hero's "lifestyle" is contrasted to the theories of some English philosophers who were highly fashionable in Dostoevsky's day and who, once again, are fashionable in ours, the "pragmatists" and the "utilitarians," those who think that the human predicament can be solved through sheer neglect or pure laissez-faire, the original free market devotees.

According to these thinkers, human beings must first be freed from religious faith. And then, if nothing else is done, if we are all left to our own devices, we will all spontaneously engage in productive activities beneficial both to ourselves and to our communities. The natural law of human behavior is *enlightened self-interest*. If it is allowed to prevail, economic, social, and political problems will all miraculously be solved.

The underground man regards all this as nonsense and, at

the end of this first part, he announces that, in the second part, which is more like a novel, he will refute utilitarianism through the sheer demonstrative force of his own life, which squarely contradicts his own self-interest. He manages to live in such a way that his interaction with other people generates the maximum amount of failure, unpleasantness, anger, humiliation, and despair for all those involved, especially himself.

And yet, the underground man fulfills all the conditions that, according to the English philosophers, should automatically lead him to seek his "enlightened self-interest." He has no religious faith; he disdains conventional morality and other "superstitions." He despises the starry-eyed idealism and altruistic benevolence that, still according to these philosophers, have always impeded the smooth functioning of "enlightened self-interest."

The underground hero is as selfish as he can possibly be, and this is precisely where his trouble lies: he cannot be sufficiently selfish. His intense mimetic desire compels him to gravitate around human obstacles of the pettiest kind. His motivation is strictly egotistical, but he is so disgusted with himself that his would-be egotism constantly turns into its own opposite and delivers him, body and soul, into the hands of petty tyrants such as the arrogant officer on the Nevsky Prospekt, or his fellow alumni from the mediocre engineering school in which Dostoevsky himself had been a student. Our hero treats these people as fearsome divinities even though, simultaneously, he sees them as complete nonentities, vastly inferior to himself in intelligence and cultural finesse.

The dramatic part of *Notes* shows us how "enlightened self-interest," at the very moment when it should triumph, is likely to be replaced by its exact opposite, a most bizarre law of "unenlightened self-enslavement," we might say, or of "obscurantist *other-interest.*"

Is not this underground law irrelevant to the vast majority of us who pride ourselves on being normal, the solid citizens of this world who have no affinities, we feel, for the antics of such mimetic freaks as Dostoevsky's grotesque creations?

The novelist anticipates this objection, and he has the underground man, his mouthpiece at this point, reject it as hypocritical. The underground is a caricature, of course, but its inmates only take to their logical extremes tendencies and propensities present in all human beings. Out of sheer timidity, and also for the purpose of keeping our own underground under control, most of us keep everything carefully hidden, even from ourselves, if not always from others. The caricatural dimension of Dostoevsky's art is also demanded by the exigencies of coherent expression; his ironic genius responds to the need for clarity by reinforcing all contrasts, by making the picture even more grotesque than it really is.

What are these tendencies and propensities which are present in all of us? Dostoevsky does not say. He cannot reach a sufficiently high level of abstraction to round up his own demonstration. He cannot put the underground in a nutshell but we can do all this for him.

We can formulate the law of the underground in terms of mimetic desire, as a relatively benign illness, no doubt, unless it is pushed to what Dostoevsky calls its logical extremes, and then it turns into what I called the obstacle addiction. What this addiction really entails is clear: underground people are irresistibly attracted to those who spurn them and they irresistibly spurn those who are attracted to them, or even those who do no more than treat them kindly.

The second part of *Notes* consists in three separate little dramas all equally grotesque, except for the third which is heart-rending as well. The first two are the story of the arrogant officer and the story of the dismal school reunion. The third is the story of the kind prostitute who tries to befriend the underground man and who is brutally rejected by him.

The first two dramas illustrate the first half of the underground law; they show that the underground man is irresistibly attracted to those who spurn him. The third drama illustrates the second half of that same law; it shows that the underground man irresistibly spurns those who are attracted to him.

Thus, exasperated mimetic desire insures a maximum amount of misfortune to those who surrender to it. When pushed far enough, the mimetic obstacle addiction compels human beings to behave in a manner diametrically opposed to anything even remotely reminiscent of their "enlightened self-interest." This, I believe, is what Dostoevsky is trying to prove.

The underground goes beyond this first demonstration. What it shows really, again and again, is that hell truly exists. Hell is not a figment of a human imagination still imprisoned in archaic thinking. Dostoevsky's interplay of obstacles and models is a terrestrial version of hell with a religious significance that still awaits definition.

We can round up Dostoevsky's demonstration by being even more reductionist than he is, with the help of mimetic desire. The theory of mimetic desire is reductionist in the extreme; its critics are right: it is reductionist with a vengeance. That is why some literary people regard it as too "systematic"; it can only imprison the fictional characters into a straitjacket, they say, a straitjacket of my own making. The function of a literary critic, these people also say, is to recapture the uniquely ineffable and inexhaustible *je ne sais quoi* with which great novelists endow the lives of their characters; he must suggest the infinite richness of a pure and noble work of art....

There is something true in this objection, and it is the straitjacket. The word is a good one to express not what I myself am doing to the underground man but what he is doing himself. He is in a straitjacket, to be sure, but not one of my own making. He got into it himself and he made it himself, or rather Dostoevsky made it for him. In this story, Dostoevsky is not yearning for some ineffable and inexhaustible *je ne sais quoi*. He seeks to convey a much starker reality, a psychological life so impoverished that it generates an incredible amount of repetitive and mechanical behavior.

Exacerbated mimetic desire is not about the richness of life, to be sure, but about the same impoverishment Dostoevsky is talking about. Much of the best twentieth-century fiction follows Dostoevsky's lead and is even more impoverished, Samuel Beckett for instance. Fiction itself becomes "reductionist," I say, and the trend begins with *Notes from the Underground*. Mimetic desire and the obstacle/model obsession finally enable us, I believe, to formulate rigorously the law of this self-impoverishment when it is realistically portrayed, as in Dostoevsky.

Even though the underground hero occasionally talks about his freedom and he is free, indeed, in the sense that no one can prevent him from impoverishing his own life, he is very much aware that he always reacts to the stimulus of other people in exactly the same predictable way. He behaves like an automaton. As a result, his life, in spite of its constant upheavals, is ultimately monotonous and repetitive. The real question is whether or not the principle of *repetition* at work in the underground is captured by the mimetic theory.

What Dostoevsky says to the laissez-faire philosophers is that, in a world as empty of transcendence as ours now is, if people are left to their own devices, many of them will choose the underground. If the novelist is right, the tepid blandness of English utilitarianism, even at its most enlightened, cannot compete with the underground because, crazy as it seems, the underground often is *the law of our own desire*.

☙

The refutation of enlightened self-interest is inseparable from the social, historical, and religious preoccupations of Dostoevsky. When religious faith recedes in the modern world, human beings no longer look up to the transcendental causes that, until then, had dominated their lives. Human beings become more rational, they feel, and, in many respects, they are right. Scientific and technical progress depend wholly on the precise and patient observation made possible by the shift of our attention from the heavenly to the earthly.

Once we are deprived of transcendental guideposts we must trust our subjective experience. Whether we like it or not, we are little Cartesian gods with no fixed reference and no certainty outside of ourselves.

Since modern man has no way of knowing what is going on beyond himself, since he cannot know everything, he would become lost in a world as vast and technically complex as ours, if he had really no one to guide him. He no longer relies on priests and philosophers, of course, but he must rely on many other people nevertheless, more people than ever as a matter of fact. They are the *experts,* the people more competent than we are in innumerable fields of endeavor.

The role of our subjective experience, therefore, is more restricted than it seems. All it can hope to do, really, when we are in trouble, is to direct us to the right *experts.*

The modern world is one of experts. They alone know what is to be done. Everything boils down to choosing the right expert. In the eyes of the eternal husband, the eternal lover is one such expert, however strange it may seem at first. It should seem less strange now than a hundred years ago. Nowadays, indeed, we have experts even in sentimental life and love making.

I observed before that the hero's choice of his wife's lover as the model of his own erotic life is supremely rational in the Cartesian and modern sense of an exclusive reliance on an individual's purely subjective experience. Our man has learned the hard way who, in matters erotic, the real expert is. It is not he, obviously; it is the eternal lover, and he behaves accordingly. He does not conform to social decorum and conventional morality; he does not follow some religious precepts. To the bitter end, he sticks to the lessons of his own subjective experience.

A rationality torn from its religious moorings surrenders its total but incompetent liberty into the hands of experts so competent that their expertise must prevail. Our attention is focused so narrowly on our immediate surroundings that we lose all sense of the wider context, of the broader picture. Our balance becomes precarious and our gait seems unsteady, a little Frankenstein-like. That is why we must cling to experts.

Our cult of experts is really one with the underground fascination for the obstacle/model of mimetic rivalry. It verges on archaic man's magical faith in terrifying idols. Having repudiated religion in order to be more rational, modern man comes full circle and, in the name of a superior rationality, embraces a rational and technical form of irrationality.

If we envisage all human behavior from a great distance, we will observe that the strange evolutions of the eternal husband can be subsumed under the label of primitive religion just as well as under the label of subjective rationality. He treats the eternal lover like a ferocious sexual idol that must be propitiated and occasionally blackmailed into dispensing some favors. To that end he sacrifices all the women in his life. From the perspective of this demonic religiosity, the death of Liza is most significant. If I had to rewrite my own long essay on Dostoevsky, I would emphasize this extremely important event.

As a result of giving up transcendence, individual pride increases, and the higher it rises, the less willing it is to humble itself, to yield any particle of its self-sovereignty. Sooner or later, this pride must encounter the tiny little stone, the puny obstacle that it will turn into a major stumbling block. This idea of an obstacle toward which we are constantly drawn, however much it hurts, is present in the Gospels. Jesus' own word, *skandalon,* or stumbling block, designates the very same mechanism as the model/obstacle of mimetic rivalry.

The more our ego-centeredness increases, the more likely it is to turn into an underground "other-centeredness" that is not "altruistic" in the slightest, even though it often masquerades as altruism. Mimetic desire is failed selfishness, impotent pride that generates the worshipful imitation of idols unrecognized as such, because they are hated as much as they are revered. The modern world insidiously brings back forms of self-enslavement from which Western society had largely escaped during the Christian centuries.

The more Dostoevsky explores the underground, the more aware he becomes of this dark and "satanic" dimension of modern life. In *The Demons* and *Brothers Karamazov* he explicitly interprets the fascination for obstacle/models as demonic possession and the psychology of the underground turns to demonology. This is no surrender to irrationality but a denunciation of it.

Social norms and restraints exist for the purpose of suppressing and moderating mimetic rivalry. The revolutionary spirit arises in an already half-disintegrated social order, one in which these norms and restraints are being relaxed and mimetic rivalries are very much on the increase. The revolutionary mystique originates in the victims of this situation, the obstacle addicts, who blame their own discomfort on the restrictions which the social order traditionally imposed upon individual behavior. The revolutionists pursue the complete destruction of this order with a passionate intensity of purpose.

Far from alleviating mimetic rivalries, the gradual loosening of the social order exasperates them. This is the reason why revolutionists never find any personal relief in the social and political "permissiveness" of prerevolutionary periods. Their desire for revolution redoubles and becomes "radicalized."

If we project our own mimetic tangles upon society as a whole, the more entangled we are, the more rigid and tyrannical the social order will appear to us, even if, in reality, it is collapsing. To revolutionists of the Dostoevskyan type, the more feeble society becomes, the more oppressive and repressive it seems.

This whole paradoxical process is the real subject of *The Demons*. To those who do not believe that the paradox is real, Dostoevsky's critique of the revolutionary mystique appears unfair, excessive, and far-fetched. Shigalyov, a minor character in *The Demons*, seems a good example of this supposed Dostoevskyan heavy-handedness. This radical theorist thinks that the only effective road to total freedom is total despotism. Whatever the revolution may do to insure total freedom, it will end up with its opposite. This is what Shigalyov discovers and, instead of prudently minimizing his embarrassing discovery, he embraces it wholeheartedly; he boldly makes it the centerpiece of his own program! As Richard Pevear observes: "Here we have the voice of the demonic idea in its pure state."*

Does not Shigalyov confirm those critics who dismiss *The Demons* as an unfair caricature of the sincere revolutionists with whom the author was associated in his youth? The character is certainly alien to factual observation. No nineteenth-century revolutionist has ever advocated despotism. Shigalyov is a slanderous creation invented for purely polemical purposes.

This character is fictional, no doubt, but what kind of a fiction is he? Obviously not the pure and gratuitous kind in which our literary critics so passionately believe. As fiction, he must be regarded as impure, since he alludes to something quite real, but not to revolutionary theory, which he distorts. He really alludes to something that even our most

*Richard Pevear, introduction to Fyodor Dostoevsky, *Demons* (New York: Knopf, 1994), xix.

sublime theorists can no longer entirely disregard, at the end
of a century with so many revolutions in it: revolutionary
reality.

Almost in the wink of an eye, after the Russian revolution, the total freedom proclaimed by the Bolsheviks
was metamorphosed into total servitude. This unexpected
metamorphosis also occurred not merely in some of the
countries which were unfortunate enough to have commu-
nist régimes thrust upon them, but in all of them without a
single exception. In the light of this fact, of these many facts
rather, Shigalyov acquires a prophetic dimension which is
unquestionable. There are very few unambiguous examples
of fulfilled historical prophecy anywhere in human history.
Shigalyov is one.

Dostoevsky was writing quite a few years before the
events that would confirm his pessimistic view of the forthcoming Russian revolution. How could he convey his mis-
givings in a work of fiction? Since the main revolutionary
activity going on at the time was theorizing, he had to
distort revolutionary theory just enough to make what he
regarded as its real implications obvious. He had to invent
Shigalyov.

Genuine prophecy always sounds a little indecent to those
whose minds are closed to its truth. A real prophet has to
make do with the material provided by his own historical
period, the very same material that leads all his contemporaries to conclusions completely opposed to his own. Was
it not indecent, in 1871, to suggest that the sincere and politically correct Russian revolutionists would end up with
Stalin and Beria?

Shigalyov is a revolutionist more honestly deluded than
most and armed with the implacable logic of an eternal hus-

band. We can well imagine that such a man might have stumbled upon the real consequences of his own principles and naively spelled them out for the benefit of fellow activists. Like many comic creations, Shigalyov is a little implausible, to be sure, but very little really, and, in view of the great prophetic truth he enables his creator to express, even a much higher degree of implausibility, in this character, would still deserve our unstinted admiration.

Professional historians do not like to acknowledge prophecy. They keep warning each other against the prophetic temptation. And I can well understand why. If we cannot recognize our own prophets even after they have been proved right, we are well advised, no doubt, to abstain from prophecy altogether.

Why did it take so little time for freedom to disappear after the Russian and other twentieth-century revolutions? The truth is that, as a rule, the original revolutionists and their successors did not merely resign themselves to the Shigalyovian paradox. In the name of liberty, they actively planned and organized the suppression of all liberties. They had not foreseen this particular kind of "historical necessity," but, when it came, they adjusted to it with the greatest of ease. All along, they must have been more Shigalyovian than anyone, except for Dostoevsky, ever realized.

As long as the Soviet Union had not collapsed, it was such a formidable historical reality that, even though discredited as an ideology, it retained the prestige of a great power, of a superpower as we love to say, pursing our lips with sensuous relish. (The people primarily interested in politics are rarely as indifferent to power as they claim to be.) To "specialists" and "experts," communism was a mistake all right, but so gigantic that even its most severe critics handled it with respect. There was still a vague fear or, in some quarters, a vague hope that the historical "necessity" of Marxism had not been disproved. A leftist version of the one-thousand-year Reich was still floating in the air.

Dostoevsky would not have been impressed. He foresaw the tremendous destructiveness of the forthcoming revolution but he never took it seriously from a spiritual and intellectual standpoint. To him it was an avatar of the underground, more ridiculous than authentically tragic. The final demise of the superpower proved him right once again. It was not the grandiose apocalypse which respectful Western historians would have expected, no doubt, had they been able to predict this collapse, if only a few years before it actually occurred; it was something that, except for some wild Russians such as Dostoevsky, neither friends nor foes had anticipated. And it happened in the same furtive and rapid manner as underground obsessions when they finally go away, not with a bang but with a whimper. Communism fizzled out in no time at all. Suddenly everybody was thinking about something else.

&

Should we disregard Dostoevsky because of his reactionary opinions? Contrary to what many people realize, he was a very "modern" man, deeply influenced by the spirit of his age until very late in his life. He was highly vulnerable to the scientistic and materialistic case against religion. He lived in the period when "scientific materialism" was triumphant and, even though, in his later life, he badly wanted to be a real Christian, genuine religious faith kept eluding him. This was the worst, perhaps, of his many thorns in the flesh.

Since he fully understood the negative usefulness of re-

ligion as a social prop against anarchy and chaos but was
personally unable to believe, his was the mood, obviously,
which makes reactionary politics a real temptation.

In his great period, his embrace of the Russian Slavophils
and traditionalists was as uncritical, in some respects, as
his former embrace of their opponents. He was far from
immune to the oscillation between extremes that characterizes the modern psyche. He was almost as mimetic as his
underground characters.

Like some Russians writers of our own time, notably
Solzhenitsyn, Dostoevsky did not respect the democratic
spirit as much as it deserves and he did not realize that, in
spite of their anti-Christian tendencies, the Western democracies are deeply rooted in the Christian tradition.

Just as many Russians and Europeans nowadays deplore
the servile imitation of everything American in their own
countries, Dostoevsky deeply resented the servile imitation
of everything Western that dominated the Russia of his time.
His reactionary leanings were reinforced by the smugness
of the West, already boasting of its great "advance" over
the rest of humanity, which was then called "progress." The
West was almost as vulgar as it is today, already confusing
its very real material prosperity with a moral and spiritual
superiority that it did not possess.

In his satire of the West and of a Westernized Russia,
Dostoevsky can be hilariously funny, but he can also be excessive and unjust. Had he been a Westerner and a political
scientist, this flaw in his thinking might have been fatal, but
he was a Russian, and his bias, when it influences his work,
is not difficult to spot.

Dostoevsky at his best is not reactionary. He perfectly
understood that Russia was in desperate need of reforms

and that tsarist autocracy plus the ultra-nationalistic orthodox church could not provide lasting answers to the
problems of his day.

Before we dismiss Dostoevsky for political reasons, we
must never forget that, even though his ferocity against
those we still call revolutionists was exemplary, he was not
gentle either with those who now call themselves conser-
vatives, the original free marketeers, the true founders of
laissez-faire economics.

The resiliency of Western democracies in the past, their
ability until now to resist the totalitarian threats that en-
gulfed Russia for so long, are no guarantee for the future.
The current wave of underground symptoms in our society
is amazingly reminiscent of Dostoevsky.

When we compare our two worlds, his and ours, the
striking thing is not how much more clever, modern,
"advanced," and "complex" we are compared to late
nineteenth-century Russia, but how stupefyingly similar.
What would Dostoevsky say about our "multicultural"
universities, our dismal sexual "liberations," our radical
feminists forcing their "all-inclusive" versions of the Bible
down the throat of meekly submissive Christian churches?
We do not have to ask; we only have to read *The Demons*.
We are living a permanent remake of Dostoevsky's most
prophetic novel, down to the silent complicity of our élites
and the universal appetite for scandals, so richly fed by
our media.

When Western humanists first encountered Dostoevsky,
they mistook him for a relic from the days of Ivan the Terrible. "He is too Russian for us," they complained. Little
did they know that, one century later, this "superlatively
bad writer" as someone said — no, it was not Nabokov,

it was Lenin — would be superlatively relevant to the interpretation of a post-communist world.

The prophetic genius of Dostoevsky is not sufficiently acknowledged and studied. Ours is not a Dostoevskyan period in the sense of being hungry for the kind of warning his novels should be for us. The real reason why this warning is not heard may well be its striking relevance. When I reread *The Demons,* I cannot help wonder if our time does not turn away from Dostoevsky because it is Dostoevskyan in the underground sense, the hysterically mimetic sense.

Dostoevsky undermines our contemporary illusions not only by satirizing them mercilessly but more simply by showing that many supposedly brilliant innovations of ours, stupendously original creations, are really warmed over nineteenth-century ideas, just a little more shrill and impudent with each passing decade.

The flaws of Dostoevsky are real, to be sure, but they should not be turned into a test of political correctness. Such tests are terroristic devices really, the true purpose of which is to shunt aside a work most rewardingly alien to the conformity of our intellectual milieu. We need Dostoevsky badly and we must resist all attempts at censoring him. He is a dead white male, all right, but his work is more alive than the cultural morticians who would like to bury him.

Bibliography

Books by René Girard

Deceit, Desire, and the Novel: Self and Other in Literary Structure.
Baltimore and London: Johns Hopkins University Press, 1966.
French original: *Mensonge romantique et vérité romanesque.*
Paris: Grasset, 1961.

Dostoevski: du double à l'unité. Paris: Plon, 1963. Republished in
Girard, *Critiques dans un souterrain.* Paris: Grasset, 1976. The
text in the 1976 publication is the basis of the present translation, *Resurrection from the Underground: Feodor Dostoevsky.*

Violence and the Sacred. Baltimore: Johns Hopkins University Press,
1977. French original: *La Violence et le sacré.* Paris: Grasset,
1972.

Critiques dans un souterrain. Paris: Grasset, 1976.

*"To Double Business Bound": Essays on Literature, Mimesis, and
Anthropology.* Baltimore: Johns Hopkins University Press, 1978.

*Things Hidden since the Foundation of the World: Research Under-
taken in Collaboration with Jean-Michel Oughourlian and Guy
Lefort.* Stanford: Stanford University Press, 1987. French original: *Des Choses cachées depuis la fondation du monde: Re-
cherches avec Jean-Michel Oughourlian et Guy Lefort.* Paris:
Grasset, 1978.

The Scapegoat. Baltimore: Johns Hopkins University Press, 1986.
French original: *Le Bouc émissaire.* Paris: Grasset, 1982.

Job, the Victim of His People. Stanford: Stanford University Press,
1987. French original: *La Route antique des hommes pervers.*
Paris: Grasset, 1985.

A Theater of Envy: William Shakespeare. New York and Oxford:
Oxford University Press, 1991. The English is the original, but
the French translation appeared first as *Shakespeare: Les feux de
l'envie.* Paris: Grasset, 1990.

Quand ces choses commenceront... Entretiens avec Michel Treguer.
Paris: arléa, 1994.

The Girard Reader. Edited by James G. Williams. New York: Crossroad, 1996.

OF RELATED INTEREST

René Girard
THE GIRARD READER
Edited by James G. Williams

In one volume, an anthology of the seminal work of one of
the twentieth century's most original thinkers.

ISBN 0-8245-1609-5 (cloth), $39.95
0-8245-1634-6 (paper), $19.95

James Alison
RAISING ABEL
The Recovery of the Eschatological Imagination

"An exceptional book ... with soaring power."
— René Girard

0-8245-1565-X; $19.95

Gil Bailie
Introduction by René Girard
VIOLENCE UNVEILED
Humanity at the Crossroads

"Prophetic in its insight, breathtaking in its scope."
— Dr. Rollo May

ISBN 0-8245-1464-5; $24.95

---

*At your bookstore or, to order directly from the publisher, please send check or
money order (including $3.00 shipping for the first book and $1.00 for each
additional book) to:*

THE CROSSROAD PUBLISHING COMPANY
370 LEXINGTON AVENUE, NEW YORK, NY 10017

We hope you enjoyed Resurrection from the Underground: Feodor Dostoevsky.
If you'd like a catalogue of all our titles, please write to us.

crossroad
herder